T0329412

It's Not Just the Coffee...

Catherine de Waal

Text © Felicity Keats Morrison 2023
First Edition 2023 © umSinsi press cc
Editor Brenda George 2023
Cover design © Thariq Kader 2023

umSinsi press cc
P.O. Box 28129
Malvern
4055
KwaZulu-Natal South Africa

ISBN: 978-1-4309-0-0382
web://www.dancingpencils.co.za

This book is original and all views expressed in the book reflect the
author's beliefs. The opinions and views expressed are not those of *umSinsi
Press*. We are an independent publishing company whose sacred objective
is to provide budding authors with a platform from which their voices can be
heard. We believe in publishing information and view-points of different
cultures and from different perspectives, in fairness and recognition of our
country's wonderful diversity.

*The story is entirely fictional and the characters bear no
resemblance to anyone living or dead*

Author's Notes

This novel *It's not just the Coffee* is Catherine de Waal's eighth novel. There are three sequels in this trilogy. The first novel of this trilogy was published in 2022 and is called *It's so Much Better Here*. *It's not Just the Coffee* is the second sequel and to be published shortly is the third novel called *Nothing Happens by Chance*.

Catherine de Waal enjoys writing and her hobby is watercolour painting. She lives in KwaZulu-Natal, South Africa, on a large wooded property, inhabited by many different types of birds, and finds inspiration in nature.

Dedication

To the memory of my beloved husband

Stuart Angus Morrison

Who believed in me and my writing.

Without you, my books would never have been born.

Thank you Sam.

Acknowledgements

Catherine de Waal has used Rooi Els on the coast of the Western Cape in South Africa as the background for this book. She would like to thank the residents of this picturesque village with its vast heritage of plant species, its birds and animals, its colourful coast line and mountains for lending her their village for this purpose.

Chapter 1

It was the child-lock that did it for Vivienne Matthews. She had been in her new house in Kalk Bay for three months now and the black shiny glass-topped electric hotplate had worked perfectly. Until that morning. A morning when she really felt like a hot cooked breakfast. A morning when Steven had phoned to say that he was going to be in Paris for, at least, six more months and was she alright?

Her heart had sunk. She was alone in a seaside village still new to her with no real support system now that Steven had transferred to Paris. She had taken a deep breath and had replied that, yes, she was alright – to a degree she was. If the stove had worked and she had been able to comfort herself with nicely fried eggs, bacon, mushrooms, French toast and the usual coffee she would have taken the news better. But she had somehow put on the child-lock and *still* had no idea of how to turn it off.

She was coping well with life in general. She had got used to being in a small house on a busy street with no garden, no friends and no maid. But she had discovered watercolour painting. And Ivor Murphy.

So it was to Ivor that her mind turned. He would know what to do to get her stove working again. It was very early in the morning, a little before six am but, Vivienne had made up her mind. She had brewed the coffee and had a hurried cup as well as one breakfast rusk. Then she picked up her big sling bag, with her small sketch book

1

inside, locked the back door and this time went out via the kitchen door.

She was casually dressed in jeans and a T-shirt with a loose jacket and flat soft canvas shoes. Her short bobbed hair was undisturbed by the small cold wind that blew about her face as she walked. On the street, autumn leaves blew in the wind and a chip packet did a dance across it. Vivienne glanced at the sky ahead. The sun had not yet arisen though it was light enough to see the street ahead with the odd car that was out early.

Vivienne had half mind to sing as she walked, but half her mind was irritated with the hotplate. She quickly thought of Steven in Paris ... his phone call was mildly upsetting, though it shouldn't be. He had proposed to Mariette and she had accepted him with delight so he was engaged to be married ... no baby yet but surely there would be one, and she, the grandmother to the baby, would be far away in Kalk Bay whilst Steven and his new family were in Paris.

A roaming dog running down the pavement bumped into her and brought her back to the moment. Be happy for Steven, she thought, and concentrate on this walk.

She knew it well by now. Up the street for a few blocks then then right for a few blocks, and then she would turn left into the street in which Ivor lived.

Ivor Murphy. She thought of him. A bare three months ago he was not in her life, but now he was definitely a part of it. She wasn't sure how he felt about it, but she knew if she wanted anything, company or someone to laugh with, or to view the day and the way the bark of a tree loosened itself and dropped off, Ivor was the person she could share that with. She had a warm feeling about Ivor. He was her coach in watercolour painting in which she had come a long way and he was also now a firm friend. In fact more than a friend. In her mind anyway. Hadn't he kissed her after she'd invited him to dinner?

The simple thought of quiet observant Ivor with his large frame, twinkling hazel eyes, his beard and slightly long light brown hair with its golden glint had her being keenly aware of the morning light on the trees and the long shadows they cast, the odd bird flying overhead and the flowers that grew in the gardens of the houses she passed. She remembered several months before going for a rapid walk when she was in a really bad mood and bumping into Ivor as she had turned a corner... she had met him before in the coffee shop where his paintings were on exhibition so they had picked up on a previous very brief meeting.

Now she was in his lane, and passing the old twisty trees with textured bark. The leaves were colouring slightly, showing the onset of autumn when the leaves would drop... fall, they call it.

She was at the small wooden gate and it was still before six am. Would

Ivor be up? She imagined so. He valued every moment of every day and she wasn't nervous as she rang the bell on the gate. In fact, she was already in a better mood, and smiling as Ivor opened his house door, saw her, and hurried to the street to open the gate.

"So early, Vivienne," he quipped. "I haven't got the coffee brewing yet. Are you that keen on having a cuppa with me?"

As Ivor opened the gate, Vivienne said, "It's not just the coffee, Ivor. I can go without coffee, but I need you to tell me how to put off the child- lock on the hotplate."

Ivor looked at her and chuckled. "You mean you've walked all this way to get help on how to switch on your stove?"

Vivienne became defensive. "Steven would know, but he's in Paris. And I really need to use that hotplate."

"So you came all this way for help?" repeated Ivor, leading the way to the house. "But please come in and I'll make coffee in a jiffy. Not as good as your coffee, but it's still coffee and I'll show you how the child-lock goes on and off."

He shook his head, and smiled. "Really Vivienne, you are so capable … but this …" And he chuckled again.

Vivienne couldn't see it as that funny, but she had relaxed. She always felt better in Ivor's company even if he did tease her.

Vivienne entered his house and followed Ivor into his kitchen, which was neat with sparsely arranged glass jars for various food items. Ivor saw her looking at them and said, "I'm not a big eater and virtually a vegetarian. So I don't have a big range of goodies to offer you … just those almond cakes I freeze and buy in bulk…. And coffee. But while the kettle boils let me show you how the child-lock works."

Facing them was a black shiny glass built-in electric hot plate. "Now watch, Vivienne," said Ivor. "It's actually very simple…" He smiled as he pressed on a corner of the hotplate for ten seconds… and the child-lock went on. He pressed for another ten seconds and it went off.

"So simple, Vivienne," he said… "Do you think you can manage?" he added with a twinkle in his eye.

"Really, Ivor, now that you've shown me, of course I can easily do it. So simple when you know how." They both laughed. Not only because it was funny, but because they were enjoying one another. How special he is, thought Vivienne.

"Now let me make the coffee," said Ivor, putting coffee grains into two mugs and pouring in boiling water.

"That's just perfect," said Vivienne adding milk and sugar. Soon they were on his porch, drinking coffee and eating almond cookies.

"I haven't seen you for a week," Ivor said. "I had that art exhibition to attend in Simonstown, which went very well. I sold a number of large paintings."

"That's wonderful Ivor," said Vivienne.

"And the good and bad news is that I'll soon be going away for another week." Ivor looked at Vivienne who looked at him questioningly. "I've been asked to give a series of lectures and demonstrations at a Convention Centre in a very small seaside resort called Rooi Els an hour or so down the coast."

Vivienne had conflicting feelings. Of joy for him and of loss for her. No Ivor for another week. She had got used to seeing him every couple of days and to even painting with him in all sorts of odd places. He had an eye for the unusual.

She saw him looking at her. "That's wonderful for you, Ivor, but your art is so good," she said truthfully, "so it's no surprise people want you to demonstrate to them. You are a good teacher." She smiled, and patted him on his arm.

This time he didn't pull away but said to her seriously, "How would you like to come with me, Vivienne? I can hire a two-bedroomed cottage with its own kitchen so we can cater for ourselves. I will be out in the day, but you can paint or draw or just relax. Below is the sea and someone once saw a mermaid there."

Vivienne's face lit up. She did not hesitate. There was nothing she needed to stay in Kalk Bay for. No cats to feed or plants to water. A short break in another seaside town would be perfect, and to share the time with Ivor would be even better. And a *mermaid!*

"Ivor that is so very thoughtful of you," Vivienne said. "I would just love it. What can I do to contribute?"

He smiled. "Well, you can make that early morning coffee, and bring your own special mix of coffee... and perhaps make breakfast." He smiled. "Bacon and eggs and mushrooms and French toast is what I like."

"And just what I wanted to make this very morning," said Vivienne.

Strangely, neither Ivor nor Vivienne seemed in a hurry to get on with their day. For Vivienne, it would mean walking home and making breakfast and then ...

"Oh, Ivor," she said, "I've been spending a lot of time studying that book on big brush watercolour painting, and not only studying it, but trying some of what the author teaches in the book. I've had a great time puddling with paint."

She smiled at Ivor.

He looked at her and answered seriously, "Did you feel any of your puddles make good paintings?"

Vivienne had stopped smiling.

"I'm surprised, Ivor. I tried misty landscapes and the next day when they had dried, there were some lovely misty effects with slightly darker trees. That big brush is amazing."

"Yes, Vivienne, it is, and I'm pleased you are noticing you are getting effects that could work well in a painting.

I think the week in Rooi Els will give you a new perspective on painting on site. What do you think?"

Vivienne said earnestly, "The whole idea is perfect." She looked at him, caught his eye and smiled. "I'm so sorry I wasn't very friendly when we first met in that coffee shop ...you are so special." At saying that, she felt embarrassed. "Sorry, Ivor, but you have lifted me to a new level of myself."

Ivor leaned back slightly in his chair. He looked more relaxed than he had done a few minutes previously. "Then the feeling is mutual, Vivienne. I must admit I felt so insecure about asking if you would like to come with me and share a cottage." He looked at her and smiled into his beard. "I must admit that helping you, even with the child-lock," he chuckled, "has put colour into my life, too." Then he added, "Yes, I get colour from my paintings, but just your presence is something I enjoy."

They both laughed at seemingly nothing at all and then spontaneously they then held hands. This felt good to Vivienne as they had both retreated into themselves after the romantic dinner she had made for him not so long ago and the kiss he had given her. Shyness, more than anything, she surmised. However, Vivienne noticed that his big warm hand held her hand for quite a long time. *What is happening between us Vivienne wondered? Were they both too scared to go forward too soon and yet both of them wanted to, she could tell.*

"Well, Vivienne, maybe I come over to you tomorrow morning, say for coffee, and we discuss what we take and when we leave. By then I will have the small details sorted."

"That will be perfect," said Vivienne. "But as I am sure you have your day planned and I now know how to switch on my stove, I'll be on my way."

Back in her own small house, Vivienne smiled as she switched on the stove and saw the red numbers flicker on. Her breakfast was perfect and she ate it with a light heart. Then, after she had cleaned up, she sat in the lounge with a pencil and paper and a dreamy look on her face. To list what she should take to cook, to plan her unfolding life in a new village. She briefly thought of Steven and she was glad for him. *Happy*. She thought again of Ivor and how he had helped her to paint atmospheric paintings. *And* now this invitation to go with him on his week's teaching assignment. Where would it lead to in their relationship?

Vivienne soon felt uplifted. The kitchen was suddenly the best kitchen she had ever had and the annoying hotplate with the child-lock was now friendly and she had cooked a breakfast she enjoyed. Yes she would cook these kinds of breakfasts, which she could vary, for Ivor if he wanted her to. She was in a kind of dreamland and then she caught herself. Goodness, the moment matters, she thought, but it's alright now because I love this home and my cheery kitchen with its yellow curtains. She smiled and was still smiling when her cell phone rang.

Nobody phoned her except for Steven in Paris and of course it *was* Steven. She was smiling as she answered the phone. Steven could hear the joy in her voice.

"Hi, Mom," he said, in a cheerful voice himself. "You sound very happy. Is there something I should know?"

Was there? She didn't know quite what to tell Steven so she brushed it off and said, "Just a developing idea…if it comes to anything, I'll tell you, but for now it's too nebulous."

She could almost see Steven nodding his head as he said, "Ok Mom, I understand. I also have some nebulous news of my own that perhaps I should wait a bit to tell you." He hesitated.

Vivienne was all of a sudden suspicious and also wanted to know. Something was up. Something big. *What was it?*

Then Steven said, "It's possible that Mariette is pregnant."

Vivienne's joyous day disappeared. Her son with a baby and not yet a wife. What was happening?

All her disappointment and insecurities where Steven was concerned surfaced. All together. Steven on the other end of the phone, waited for her to say something.

"Well, Mom, aren't you pleased you will have a grandchild?" he eventually asked.

Vivienne swallowed hard. She did her best to keep the light tone in her voice, but failed miserably. So she said instead, "That's wonderful for you, Steven. What did Mariette's parents say?"

"She hasn't told them yet, Mom. You are the only person besides us who knows and it isn't definite, just a possibility." Steven hastened on. "It's all new, to us but Mariette is the girl I've always dreamed of so I am happy and so is she. We will deal with whatever we have to when we have to." He hesitated for a moment and then in a whisper said, "I'm ringing off now, Mom. Her father is coming into the room."

Vivienne didn't even have time to say goodbye and he had switched off his cell. I wonder how he's really feeling, she thought. But her own thoughts were in a turmoil. She couldn't get back to enjoying the moment and having a peaceful mind. Gloomily, she noticed her thoughts were all over the place. Her heart was in her stomach and she felt miserable. Ridiculous when only a short while ago she had been joyous!

She knew there was one thing to get her back on track and it wasn't watching her thoughts. It was locking up and taking a walk to see Lady Lavender …

Lady Lavender lived in a very old fisherman's cottage in between the high hills and the sea. Vivienne had found a wonderful ear in the psychic when she first had arrived in Kalk Bay and was so upset…thinking she had made a mistake in selling up and moving here. Lady lavender had assured her that there were no accidents, that she was meant to. She had learned a lot from Lady Lavender.

Vivienne instinctively knew that Lady Lavender would help her to calm down. To get back to being content with her life. And she knew she needed to do this before tomorrow morning when Ivor visited to talk about the week at Rooi Els. There was a mermaid there he had said. She smiled. *Would she see a mermaid at all?*

But that reminded her that she had to watch her thoughts and to watch where she was going, so at least she was not too much of a mental muddle when she arrived at Lavender Cottage. As usual, she found her way down the twisty path between small houses and trees until she came to the sudden view of the old fisherman's cottage with lavender and roses in the garden. Vivienne saw the big brass knocker on the door and smiled. She fairly frequently visited Lady Lavender, but in those days she was in a calm mood and without any special worries.

Today was different and she was still feeling agitated as she knocked on the door. Almost instantly it opened and there was the tall angular figure of Lady Lavender, with her black hair and gimlet eyes, dressed today in a long dress of leaf-green.

"It's not spring time yet," she said to Vivienne with a smile. "I was expecting you. Please come in."

Lady Lavender always knew when she was on the way.

"You know the rules, Vivienne," she said. "Kitchen first – ginger tea and today's biscuits are lemon drops. Made with lemon peel grated into them."

Lady Lavender's unusual home was like a second home to Vivienne now and she followed her host into the kitchen and sat on a stool while Lady Lavender poured boiling water into two delicate china cups, in which she had put a few pieces of raw ginger.

"Please help yourself to biscuits, Vivienne, and now with the honey in these cups we are all set. I can see you have much to tell me."

Vivienne nodded, following Lady Lavender into her large lounge. In it and occupying one of the two comfortable large chairs was a very large black cat with staring green eyes and bristling white whiskers.

"Captain," she said to the cat, "we have a visitor. Please sit, Vivienne, and take a sip of tea before you talk… I see you need to gather yourself first."

Yes, she did. Her thoughts were flying to her peaceful life in Cowies Hill, to Steven, who had let her down by going to live in Paris and to getting engaged and now having made his fiancé pregnant. She felt discarded –forgotten and close to tears.

The tea helped. She sat for a half a minute sipping it and breathing hard. Lady Lavender was watching her.

"That's perfect, Vivienne," she said. "Breathing will help to calm your thoughts. When you are ready you can tell me what brought you here today."

Vivienne almost smiled. How well Lady Lavender knew her. "It was Steven again," she said.

"Your son who has gone to live in Paris."

"Yes, that son."

"What has he done now?" asked Lady Lavender.

Vivienne hurried to reply.

"I was feeling uplifted just before he phoned. But one sentence from him has thrown me into turmoil. The past keeps jumping up and I'm totally miserable."

"Well, not totally," corrected Lady Lavender.

"Alright, a bit of me is happy to be here with you, Lady Lavender, because you help me so much just by listening to me."

"Yes, I'm waiting to hear," said Lady Lavender.

"Steven had news that upset me terribly. He thinks his fiancé is pregnant." Vivienne stopped, almost gasping as she said this.

She noticed a small smile on Lady Lavender's face.

"And you are not happy for them?" she asked.

Vivienne felt confused, so she shook her head. "No, I'm not, Lady Lavender. Steven is not yet married and they have not yet told her parents."

Lady Lavender shook her head.

"There's a great saying you might remember, Vivienne. For short it is MYOB. Or mind your own business. In other words, your son is an adult and able to make his own decisions...he's already shown you that in choosing to live in Paris. What you need to do is to step aside and let him and Mariette decide what they are going to do about their lives. If you don't interfere, they will confide in you."

Vivienne shook her head. "This is so hard for me, Lady Lavender. I was so close with my son. We shared everything."

"And don't you think he is sharing with you now?"

"Well, I guess so," said Vivienne reluctantly.

"Of course, he is. He said they haven't yet told her parents, but they have told you. That in itself is a great compliment."

Vivienne took a deep breath. "I suppose it is," she said.

"And you need to remember that you don't come into the picture, Vivienne. Just stand aside and let them deal with the situation. Listen, but don't judge. Do you find that difficult?"

"Extremely," said Vivienne, "which is why I came to see you. I felt as if I was drowning in my own misery."

"Well stop and be aware," said Lady Lavender. "Where are you now?"

Vivienne took a deep breath and shut her eyes.

"That's right," said Lady Lavender. "If you close your eyes and watch your thoughts you'll get that peaceful no-thought head, don't you remember?"

Vivienne had forgotten. She sighed again, kept her eyes shut and watched her thoughts. They were turbulent at first then, surprisingly, they slowed down and then they were gone.

"And when you are not thinking anything at all, stay in that stillness Vivienne. And beam peace, harmony, abundance and good positive things into your mind. These will ground you and keep you safe. Do remember your lessons, Vivienne."

Vivienne sat with her eyes shut for much longer than necessary. But she was enjoying this peaceful no-thought state she was currently in.

"Don't think, Vivienne. Thinking is the wrong thing to do. Awareness is the right thing, awareness of your surroundings and you in the moment with your gratitude for everything."

Vivienne was suddenly aware that she was indeed grateful; grateful for Ivor's invitation and she immediately smiled at Lady Lavender.

"I haven't told you the good news," she said, "which I might have spoiled if I had stayed in the state I was in. But Ivor..."

"The artist."

"Yes, the artist ... has a commission to teach beginners watercolour painting an hour down the coast at a Convention Centre and he asked me if I would like to join him... he suggested he would rent a two-bedroomed cottage and I could stay with him."

"Marvellous idea, Vivienne," said Lady Lavender. "You see, you are moving to a new dimension and if you can control your emotions and your thoughts, you will be lifted high onto the next level. Nice work, Vivienne."

Vivienne was suddenly out of the gloom she'd been in and entering into a feeling of everything being just so right.

"And have you told your son?" asked Lady Lavender.

Vivienne was embarrassed.

"No," she said.

"You see," said Lady Lavender, "that is the correct thing to do. You are learning to MYOB very nicely. It is your business, but a lot of Ivor's too and he might not be ready for you to talk to your son about it. Even if it is a case of an artist and his pupil sharing a cottage. Keep a silent mouth, Vivienne ... and grateful heart. And see what joy transpires."

Vivienne noticed the black cat had stood up and was stretching. She smiled. "Captain is telling me it is time to leave," she said. "And as always, your wisdom has put me back in to a good place in myself. Thank you, Lady Lavender."

Vivienne stood up, followed closely by Captain who saw her out of the house. She could feel Lady Lavender's eyes on her from the window in the lounge.

Chapter 2

The next morning, Vivienne heard the car door shut and the ping as the electric alarm went on. She felt her heart leap as she heard the leisurely footsteps outside then the knock on her door.

This time she opened it immediately, to be greeted by Ivor with his twinkling hazel eyes and a smile that disappeared into his shaggy brown beard.

The smell of coffee was strong.

"It's not just the coffee I've come for," he quipped. "And how are you, Vivienne?"

Vivienne replied, "Very well, thanks, Ivor. Please come in." She stood aside and ushered him into the kitchen.

Shortly after, with the back door shut and locked and equipped with a cup of coffee and a plate of Vivienne's foam biscuits, they repaired to the lounge and seated themselves in front of the coffee table, on which there were a sheaf of paper

"You've given up painting and taken up writing," Ivor quipped.

Vivienne laughed. "No, Ivor, I've been making notes of what to bring...what to eat, what painting equipment, what clothes. And I'd really like to know where we are going, so I can prepare properly."

"Let's start with where," said Ivor.

"It's a coastal village beyond Gordon's Bay and not as far as Hermanus. It's called Rooi Els. It is like a wildlife sanctuary in that it has more rare plants than most places in the world. It has a colony of protected penguins, and is situated on a rocky untidy coastline that is part of the Western Cape … from there, across the wide expanse of False Bay, you can just see the tip of the Cape … Cape Point. It's very misty, because of the distance.

"It was declared a village in June, 1948. And shortly after building was stopped in certain parts. Where we are going is on a large tract of virgin earth, with proteas and wild heather and many other beautiful flowering plants. And a beautiful view of the sea. As well as lots of rocks." Ivor laughed at this. "Behind the property, visible from most parts of Rooi Els, is a very large strange- shaped rock you could call a mountain. It's made of reddish rock.

"Our path leads off the main road, twists down this large tract of uninhabited land to a beautiful Convention Centre built by some far-sighted people, who felt that the nature that's all around would inspire people like artists, botanists, and hikers. So, behind the Centre, there is a cluster of buildings for the staff, and in front of it are four weekend cottages, each equipped for two or three people to share. I've been there and you'll love it.

"So that's the where…. From the Convention Centre, one looks down onto rolling waves and large rocks and a very blue ocean…It's a steep walk and it would be better if you waited for me when I am free to come with you."

Vivienne had been listening and imagining it in her mind's eye. She felt excited though she didn't say anything as Ivor continued.

"You'll find plenty to do as an artist, just around the cottage, or a short distance in any direction. There is the mountain behind, the sky with lovely thick curly clouds above, and there are huge unusually shaped rocks, plants of all kinds, flowers and birds and, of course, the famous baboons ..."

Vivienne was excited and said, "You paint such a vivid picture I know I'm going to love my time there."

Ivor continued, "And you'll love the accommodation."

Vivienne said, "And if the cottages are self-catering, I take it there are cooking facilities and a fridge. And do I need to take plates and cutlery? That sort of thing ... also, what do you like to eat? I know you are a semi-vegetarian. Does that mean you don't eat eggs fish and chicken?"

Ivor patted Vivienne's arm. "You are being thorough, Vivienne. Thank you, but I eat all those. I just am not a big meat-eater. There is also a restaurant attached to the Convention Centre, where I'll probably have lunch on some days with the students. There are six of them staying in the other cottages."

Vivienne was curious about the students and asked if they were young.

"Age doesn't matter with art," said Ivor. "But they are mostly retired people. Or people that haven't needed to work. Or are able to take leave." He smiled. "There are four women and two men. All about our age. And one of them says she knows me from long ago. I have no memory of her at all ... Maureen Grylke is her name."

Vivienne put that name in her memory box. Later, just out of curiosity, she'd find out how Maureen got to know Ivor.

"They are all beginners," said Ivor. "All going to learn the variety of ways they can use our favourite big brush, the hake."

Vivienne could see Ivor was getting fired up. He was passionate about his painting and he did make the hake create amazing landscapes.

Ivor continued. "Our cottage is the furthest away, but that is good. I don't like to socialize with students." He gave Vivienne a special smile. "But it's different with you," he said. "We didn't start our friendship with art ...we began by getting to know one another as friends, then the art came into it so I consider you a friend rather than a student."

"Yes, Ivor," Vivienne said. "It was a bumpy start as I know I wasn't that agreeable ..." She was serious now "...but you helping me with art has changed my life and I am truly grateful... so I am a student, too." She was earnest.

Ivor just looked at her and smiled. "You are your own person, Vivienne," he said. "And this is going to be an interesting week."

It was a few days later and Vivienne was dressed in jeans, a turquoise T-shirt with a navy jacket She wasn't wearing a cap or a hat as she had wisely guessed that Ivor would have the sun roof down and that the wind would blow away any hat or cap. Ivor too had nothing on his head and he looked pleased when he saw Vivienne's attire..

"Ready to have the sunroof down, Vivienne, I see," said Ivor, with the usual twinkle in his hazel eyes.

"Oh yes, Ivor, the wind on my face is a wonderful sensation. Funny, I didn't used to like the wind, but, somehow, it seems to be my friend now."

"That's good to hear, Vivienne, because we might meet up with all kinds of weather. Hot, cold, wet, windy...I'll be protected, because I'll be in the Convention Centre. Do you mind being on your own?"

"Not at all, Ivor. As you said, I can sleep all day if I wish."

"Yes, and there are two identical bedrooms, Vivienne, and you can have first choice. I've been there before so I know the lay of the land. There's a large lounge with comfy sofa and chairs and even a television. A bathroom and a kitchenette with great views of the ocean. And a security gate on the front door. You can stay indoors all day if you wish. You decide when you get there. This large property is fenced in so you are safe and you may like to find a wild spot outside and either sketch or paint what you see."

"I've brought the book on watercolour painting with me," she said. "I can read it and put into practice what I read."

Ivor nodded. "I can share with you what my lessons will be about, but you are way ahead of what I'll be teaching," he said.

That made Vivienne feel good – to be advancing so well that Ivor recognized it.

Soon they were on their way with the sunroof down and the breeze whipping her short hair around her face. It felt marvellous and she was suddenly so glad she'd sold up and moved to Kalk Bay. Life was opening up new opportunities.

"The coastline down here is really spectacular," said Ivor. "Lots of little inlets and we drive right along next to the sea. This is still the coastline of False Bay, on the eastern coast. Rooi Els is five kilometres past Pringle Bay, on the way to Hermanus. It is perfect in every way for the artist. On the one side, high hills and mountains and, on the other, a really rough sea, bashing great rocks, with a patch of sand too. When I'm not training, I'll walk with you in the rougher parts with rocks and high waves, but there's plenty for the artist's eye right around the cottages and the Convention Centre."

Ivor was a good driver and Vivienne felt safe as they wound along beside the sea. The scenery was natural and wild, with rocks and pink and purple heather on the one side and the glorious deep-blue sea on the other. They passed a few small settlements, where houses were grouped together and people down below were surfing or sunning themselves on the beaches. They passed Pringle Bay, well before Hermanus and, not much further on, Ivor said, "We are almost there. Next turn to the right is the driveway down to the Convention Centre. And look, you can see it with the four cottages grouped around it."

Vivienne could and felt another leap of her heart. One week here amidst rocks and heather, with mostly sky and sea as companions. She suddenly missed her quiet home at Cowies Hill where there was a small paradise of wildlife in her garden... her mind briefly travelled there and then back as Ivor was speaking. "The Saturday morning I have free, when I can spend time with you doing whatever pleases you... sightseeing, or painting or even just chatting." He smiled as he said that and Vivienne knew he would not enjoy chatting ... He continued, "But, on Saturday afternoon, there is a fun painting workshop, which you are welcome to join."

Ivor continued. "Regarding the students. Three women will share one cottage and one is on her own, and the two men will share a cottage. They are not young. But you can start painting at any age and it's a companion for life. I don't know any of them but there's that one woman who says she knows me from long ago. So, it is a new experience for me as well. As an artist it is by teaching that one improves one's art."

Vivienne digested all of that. One woman who said she knew him from long ago. It wasn't the first time he'd told her about her. She was sure Ivor would tell her more after his first training.

Now the car had turned off the tarred road and was winding down the hill through heathers and rocks towards the distant ocean and the Convention Centre with the four cottages in easy access of it.

Ivor stopped the car at the reception notice. "I'll book us in, Vivienne, and will be out with the keys shortly. We are number 8," he said. "I guess the outbuildings also have numbers." Their cottage had a neat paved path leading to it but it was further away than the other three cottages.

"Gives us a better view," said Ivor. "No dwellings in front of us. Just heather and rocks and sky and sea."

"Perfect," said Vivienne.

Ivor looked at her and she could see he was pleased with her reply. Vivienne was content to sit and look around at rough growing heathers and large grey rocks. A baboon popped its head out from behind a tree. Yes, baboons took things and could be dangerous, so one needed to respect them, she remembered, so no leaving small valuables around, like her sunglasses or paint brushes.

Vivienne looked at the Convention Centre. It had long glass windows and she could see a lounge with a cosy fire burning. Through the arch in the lounge she got a glimpse of white-clothed tables set for lunch or dinner. Off the lounge were other rooms, one of which she guessed was the demonstration room where Ivor would be training these new artists.

In a way, she wished she was part of the group but another part of her said that this was better. Less of Ivor, more quality time with him. She could be content on her own. One difficulty was that the cell phone line was virtually non-existent, because of the mountains, but in a way that was okay. Steven was away for a week and she would decide what to do about getting a decent line later on.

Soon Ivor was back holding a key. Vivienne looked at him. He radiated a feeling of contentment with his shoulders back and a slight smile on his face. He was looking up at the mountains then around about them at the heathers and large fallen rocks.

"It's perfect, isn't it?" he said as he got into the car. "Perfect to let in new energies and breathe out old ones, and perfect for the artist." He looked at Vivienne, directing her gaze to where he was looking. "So much to paint," he said. "Look at those clouds." Vivienne did. They were round, white and fluffy in a deep-blue sky. "If you make a busy sky, keep the foreground simple." Then he pointed to the shrubs and rocks around them. "You simplify these, but look at the different shades of green and look at the rocks. They too are very interesting, of different shapes and with slight variations of colour."

Vivienne's eyes followed where he was pointing.

"And then look down there, Vivienne," he said almost holding his breath. "The sea with a late-afternoon sun. Look how it backlights those waves. Even from here we can see that. There is so much to paint here." He gave a deep contented sigh then added, "Rock formations fascinate me, Vivienne. But let's go and see our accommodation. As I said, you choose first." He had started the car and they drove the short distance to the cottage and parked at the side. "So we don't spoil our view," he said. "Now, my lady, please enter and gaze upon our accommodation. I hope it is to your satisfaction."

It was. The lounge had large glass doors that looked down the slope towards the sea. And it was decorated in cool and friendly blues and turquoise. Vivienne looked at it and smiled at Ivor. "It's lovely, Ivor," she said.

"Right, now there are the two bedrooms opposite. Please look and choose." The first one Vivienne entered was decorated in daffodil yellow and she immediately felt warm and uplifted. "I like this one," she said.

"But you haven't seen the second one," objected Ivor. "Just look, anyway."

Vivienne did and it was equally charming, decorated in a refreshing green.

"Lovely for you," she said, using some of the way he quipped with her, "but I'll go with my first choice, thanks, Ivor."

"And look in the lounge," said Ivor. "There's a neat dining-room table that will be perfect if you choose to sit indoors and paint." Vivienne saw it. "And off the lounge is the kitchenette with a bar counter for easy eating," said Ivor. The kitchenette was indeed very small and the large fridge stood in a corner of the lounge just next to the bathroom.

But, all in all, it was perfect. "And it has electric light too," said Ivor, "so we are really having a fully equipped venue for us as artists who need to eat and sleep. Let me settle you in your room then you might like to unpack the food items. If you don't mind, I'd like to go to the Convention Centre and check out the venue for tomorrow's classes. Are you okay with that?"

Vivienne knew he meant – did she feel safe? Yes, she did, and if she didn't, she could always close the long glass door. Or pull the security gate across the open door.

"That's a good idea, Ivor," she said. "Let me unpack food and organize it where it's convenient. I brought along some snacks for in betweens."

"Excellent and, tonight, I'll book us into the restaurant for dinner. Tomorrow, will be time enough for you to start cooking and me to start lecturing." His deep glance into Vivienne's eyes said more than words could say and she felt a pool of warmth inside her. She just nodded at him.

As he walked up the path towards the Convention Centre, Vivienne watched him. So he thought of her as a friend primarily, a friend who he liked to paint with, not a student he was teaching. She realised that she liked that thought. These six people. including Maureen, who knew him, were his students. She was his friend who liked to paint with him. Yes, it was different and she was glad she was not with the students. She would find plenty to do on her own.

Back to the moment and start sorting the food, she told herself. Freezer items in the freezer trays of the fridge, cool items in the fridge and bread and other items like the coffee and sugar, she stored neatly on a shelf in the kitchenette. On the coffee table in the lounge, she arranged some biscuits and cheese to nibble on. She had included two bottles of white wine and even a bottle of champagne to toast the week here, she said to herself, as she looked in the kitchenette for two wine glasses.

Then she sat on an outside chair with her little sketch book and black permanent fine line pen. But she wasn't ready to sketch. Her mind was too busy. Even a thought of Steven popped into it. This was just a friendship. Did she even need to tell him anything? She shook her head. Watch my thoughts, she told herself. I think I know why Ivor walks to clear his head. Mine needs clearing. She shut her sketch book and put away her pen. Ivor was still in the Convention Centre, so she thought to take a walk and just watch her thoughts and look at her surroundings. She took a very slow walk and concentrated on what was around her. Right above her, on the other side of the road, was that odd-shaped rock that was so huge and high that it was actually a mountain. She gazed at it. There were a number of shades of red, white, silver-grey and even a deep copper colour in it. Yes, she said to herself, become the rock, think like the rock. Be the rock. Then it will be easy to sketch it.

Right now, she didn't concentrate on anything else. None of the fascinating heathers and proteas and other small pretty wild flowers, or the clouds or the sea. Just the red rocky mountain. Her mind was clear, her thoughts gone. She breathed deeply. I'm connecting with that rock, she thought, and quickly got out her sketch book. Turning her chair around and moving it to get a better view of the mountain, she sat, immersed in her drawing, just looking at the mountain and sketching without looking at what she was doing.

She was immersed in the last lines when Vivienne got the feeling that someone was watching her. She looked up and saw that Ivor had come around the corner and was standing staring at her with a strange look on his bearded face. She smiled at him, and closed her sketch book, putting it in her bag on the ground next to her.

Ivor came towards her quietly. "Vivienne you had such a rapt expression on your face," he said. "It was as if you had seen an angel."

"Maybe I did," said Vivienne. "That was such a great experience. I know now why you need a quiet head to paint. I needed a quiet head to draw that mountain."

Ivor was looking at her with serious hazel eyes. "You are becoming a true artist, Vivienne," he said, "where the art speaks to you and you respond in whatever way seems right. You were connected with that mountain, I could tell." He hesitated then, very reverently, asked, "Would you mind showing me what you drew?"

Vivienne took the small art book out of her bag and opened it at the page she had just drawn.

Ivor pulled up a second chair and sat close to her to see her drawing. His head was bent to study her drawing. His light brown hair, Vivienne noticed, definitely held a glint of gold. She smiled to herself. Would he ever tell her any of his past history, of his family, for instance? She would love to know. Maureen Gtylke came into her head, but she dismissed the thought immediately.

"It's lovely, Vivienne, very sensitive, and you have caught the essence of the rock. That is so special. Congratulations!" He put out his hand to take hers. Surprised, she took it and felt it was warm and firm. A good time to mention the champagne, she thought.

"Ivor, I don't know if you drink champagne, but I brought along a bottle just to toast our coming week in this lovely wild place... and the great sketches and paintings I'm going to do ... and your successful week as a tutor."

Ivor looked surprised as he released her hand. "Right now?" he asked.

"Why not?" she countered. "Just to wish us both well for this week and success for each of us in our own way."

Ivor smiled his pleased agreement. It took very little time to bring out the glasses and two plates with some savouries to nibble.

"It's like a dream," breathed Vivienne. Ivor, seated on the chair next to her, turned and looked at her. "All of this," she said. "But please open the champagne, Ivor, and let's make a toast to a successful week." He was smiling down at Vivienne as they clinked glasses. "To a successful week." Vivienne was remembering that by being in the happy moment one built a happy life, so she was savouring this moment with Ivor, the champagne, the sea and the peace.

"Thank you, Ivor," she said quietly.

The companionable silence that followed was more meaningful to Vivienne than any small talk. She lifted the champagne glass to her lips and was glad it was still cold. A bit later, Ivor said, "Dinner is at seven, Vivienne."

Later, she saw Ivor glance at her plain midcalf deep-blue dress appreciatively and was glad of her choice.

"You look nice," Ivor said. "Shall we walk up? A bit of exercise will be good for us both."

He shut and locked the door, then took her right arm. Vivienne felt happy to be on Ivor's arm.

As they neared the restaurant, they met up with a group of people. "My students," breathed Ivor.

"Good evening, everyone," he said, "are you ready for tomorrow?

"Yes," they chorused back.

"We are so looking forward to the lessons," said one of them. "I'm Walter and pleased to be in your group." Walter was fairly young, good looking, well built and nicely dressed, He didn't really look like an artist but one couldn't go by appearances Vivienne thought.

Ivor carried on walking with Vivienne, and once inside the reception area, booked in for dinner and was shown, by a waiter, a corner table for two. Next to their table was a long table with seating for six. The students. Vivienne wished they would not be sitting so close, but there was nothing she could do about the seating arrangements.

There were menus at each place. As Vivienne and Ivor were studying them, a woman joined them. Vivienne and Ivor looked up as she cleared her throat and touched Ivor on the shoulder. She was an attractive middle-aged woman, sexily dressed in a deep maroon garment showing a lot of bosom. She had long dark hair draped on either side of her face.

Her coal-black eyes gleamed as she looked at Ivor and said in a seductive voice, "Hello, Ivor darling. Do you remember me? I'm Maureen. Mo, you used to call me.".

Ivor looked at her with a blank expression on his face.

"I've booked to come on this painting course, especially to see you," she said. "I've been trying to catch up with you for years."

Vivienne was watching the scene and remembered Lady Lavender's recent words, MYOB. This was not her business, so she looked back down at the menu. Irresistibly, she glanced up to see Ivor looking at the woman, with bewilderment showing in his hazel eyes.

"You say I knew you?" He sounded puzzled. "I don't remember you at all."

"I didn't look like this, so you may not remember me. I was seventeen and so were you and you lived next door to me in Durban."

"Tell me more," said Ivor.

Vivienne again dropped her eyes to the menu.

"We spent a lot of special time together," she said. "Really special."

"I'm sorry I don't remember you at all," said Ivor, a touch of irritation in his voice.

"But you were dotty about painting. I'm glad to see you succeeded," said Maureen. "But your painting angered your father and he beat you badly. Don't you remember, darling? I helped you run away from home?"

Ivor was frowning now. Vivienne could see he was angry. What did all this mean?

34

"Please, madam, we are at dinner now. Can this wait for another time," he said to Maureen.

Maureen didn't look like a person who could be easily dismissed, but she did stop talking.

"Tomorrow then," she said. "I've waited years to catch up with you."

Tossing her long dark hair back, she moved away from their table and seated herself at the next table where five people were now seated and watching. Vivienne let out a mental sigh of relief. There was something disturbing about the woman, chilling even.

Ivor took a deep breath, then bent towards Vivienne. "I'm sorry about that. What have you decided on, Vivienne?" he asked as the waiter arrived to take their orders.

"I'm going for chicken schnitzels with salad and chips," she said, "and you?"

"I'll have the same," said Ivor. "And to drink?"

"A glass of white wine, please," said Vivienne.

"I'll have a glass of red wine, please," Ivor told the waiter.

Vivienne didn't like to question Ivor about the encounter. He seemed to be as unnerved by the woman as she was. It must have been very traumatic for him to have lost all memory of what the woman had spoken about, but it was not, she reminded herself, her business.

She looked at the menu and pointed to the desserts.

"I see some interesting desserts," she said. "Strawberry shortcake with cream or lemon meringue tart ... I'm not sure which."

"The strawberry shortcake for me," said Ivor, and Vivienne was relieved to see his face relaxing.

The food was good and the rest of the evening went off without incident. Ivor took Vivienne's arm again as they walked back. It was dark now and the stars were out in a navy sky. With no street lights, the firmament was just a glorious starry wonder. Vivienne breathed deeply. The air was cool with small night noises and the occasional bark of a baboon.

"It's all so special," she said.

Ivor was deep in thought and didn't reply. Vivienne hoped that Maureen hadn't opened a Pandora's box of some kind.

Then they were at their cottage and Ivor was unlocking the door.

"Thanks. Ivor, that was a lovely meal," said Vivienne.

"It's still early," said Ivor. "We are sharing the bathroom. Do you need to bath or shower now?"

"No," said Vivienne. "I'll be up early tomorrow morning before coffee, and shower then, but for now, I'd like to put on a warm wrap and sit outside and look at the stars and listen to the night noises."

"That is a great idea," said Ivor with a touch of relief in his voice. "I'll join you."

So, each wrapped warmly, they sat together outside on chairs, doing nothing but looking at the firmament above and listening to the noises that came from the dark landscape. Vivienne smiled in the dark. This was perhaps the right way to end this first day of the painting retreat.

As Vivienne lay in bed, she thought how she had changed. From the introverted woman tied to her son, she had been forced to let him go. She was not so conscious of being correct and dressing formally most of the time. She was now comfortable in jeans and a T-shirt, at least in the day time, though dinner did call for a change of clothing. She realised that she could laugh at herself, something she'd found hard to do before, and felt intensely grateful for this new chapter in her life. Her husband had passed away twenty years ago, and was not holding her back. Ivor didn't know much about her, and she knew just the little he had told Lady Lavender, that he had been interested in painting from the age fourteen when he had wanted to paint red clouds ... He had mentioned a penniless time when he struggled as an artist. But where had Maureen come in?

Quickly, she reminded herself, it was none of her business. Tomorrow Ivor would hear more from Maureen. She hoped she wouldn't disrupt his painting class.

Chapter 3

Vivienne was up, showered and with the coffee on when Ivor surfaced from his room and came into the kitchen. He looked more relaxed and even gave Vivienne a cursory hug.

"It isn't just the coffee," he said, "but it does smell good."

"And I'm sure it will taste good," said Vivienne, putting a steaming cup down in front of him.

"I think I'll drink it outside," Ivor said. "Have to get my mind empty for today's course." He said it in a way that seemed to say he had forgotten about Maureen and the incident at dinner.

"Yes, I'll cook breakfast and it won't be long," said Vivienne.

Soon there were smells of a hot breakfast. Vivienne found a toaster and made toast. She put knives and forks, the butter and marmalade and salt and pepper all on the bar counter then called out, "Breakfast's ready, Ivor."

Ivor had on a red-and-blue checked shirt and loose baggy pants. He had a briefcase of paints, papers and books and after breakfast and a second cup of coffee, he gently ruffled Vivienne's hair and said, "Wish me luck, Vivienne," but he smiled as he said that and Vivienne laughed. Ivor would cope with whatever the day held for him.

Vivienne watched Ivor's big frame as he walked easily out of the cottage and up the path. For a moment, Vivienne thought of the disturbing Maureen; there was something scary and unnerving about her. Vivienne could not quite put her finger on it. She had never met a woman as confident of her effect on men as she had been. She had acted as if Vivienne did not even exist. She had honed in on Ivor as deliberately as an eagle does its prey, claws outstretched.

Then, shaking herself, Vivienne forced herself to dismiss her. She had learned many lessons from Lady Lavender in keeping her attention on what she was doing and not letting it wander to things that didn't concern her. What did concern her first was clearing up after breakfast then deciding well in advance what was to be for supper. She had a frozen spinach and feta casserole and that, with some boiled new potatoes with butter could make an easy supper. That need only happen late in the afternoon. The day was hers once her domestic chores were over.

No one was around. *What to do?* She sighed as she stood looking out.

Far below was the blue sea with its frills of white surf. Above was the blue endless sky with just slight clouds in it. She moved to get a better view of the mountain behind her. There was that interesting mountain she had already drawn. It still fascinated her. The strata were all lying longitudinally. But, for now, she and the rock had had a session. What else might she do today?

Perhaps do what Ivor did. Clear her head so that she wasn't thinking. Take a walk with an empty mind and just be aware of everything as she walked. That seemed like an idea. She picked up her sketch book and pen, locked the cottage and pocketed the key. She wore jeans and a T-shirt and soft easy canvas shoes. Today, she had a small hat on her head. The brim kept the sun out of her eyes. She began to walk. Away from the cottage. Not too far, she told herself. But just far enough to get an empty head. A no-thought head. She observed as she walked the pretty flowering wild flowers. A rock caught her eye. A rock that looked almost human.

No one was around and it was really quite stupid, she thought, as she greeted the rock.

"Hullo, Rock," she said. "You look interesting. And I think we should share some time together. What do you think? You appear to be like an old man in a cloak with a firm and determined chin." She smiled at the rock.

"Mr Rock, I'm going to take a good look at you and then I'm going to shut my eyes for five minutes and when I open them, I'm going to draw. . .. your essence, if not you as you stand there."

So she closed her eyes. The sun beat down on her, and a small wind tickled her ears. But she sat.

Of course, the rock couldn't answer, but Vivienne felt the rock appreciated her taking notice of it. *Weren't we all connected?* Hadn't Lady Lavender told her that? So perhaps the rock might let her get in touch with her own inner wisdom just in being silent and sharing herself with the rock. She squatted on a smaller rock opposite it, and looked hard at the rock. It had been worn away by weather and it did look like an old man in a cloak.

Then she said aloud, "I'm just going to look at you and let the pen draw your essence. Thank you, Mr Rock." And this is just what she did.

Sitting there staring at the rock, she held the sketch pad in one hand whilst the other hand traced fine lines on the paper. Vivienne had read in a book somewhere that this method did capture the essence ... not looking to see what she was doing, not thinking, just looking and letting her hand trace whatever it liked on the paper.

She probably sat looking at the rock and not at her hand or the drawing on the paper for perhaps twenty minutes. When she felt she had drawn what mattered, she gave a deep sigh and said to the rock ... "That was the most uplifting time I've ever spent. I was on another plane, or so it felt like it." As she lifted her eyes, she was sure she saw coloured geometric lights in the air surrounding the rock. She closed her eyes and shook her head and when she opened her eyes the coloured geometric forms had vanished and she was looking at the rock.

"That's still the most amazing time I've ever had," she told the rock, now feeling as if it was an old friend. She dropped her eyes to look at what she had drawn.

It was nothing like the rock at all but, in some way, there was something etheric or mystical about what she had drawn. It was not something one would want to throw away even if it didn't look like the rock. Vivienne sat for perhaps another half an hour, with an empty mind, clear of all thoughts and she knew a feeling of great peace, such as she had never known before. To keep this peace, she reminded herself to be aware of where she was and to observe everything very clearly and not to think. So she idled her way amongst the plants and smiled as she surprised a baboon resting under a tree.

Goodness, it was nearing noon and what had she done? She had become quiet and peaceful, that's what …but of painting, she had done nothing.

But it didn't seem to matter.

Vivienne strolled on, getting closer to the cottage, and viewing the sea below with the white foam of breakers dashing against rocks. Time for a quick snack and then maybe a short rest. Though she had done nothing, she felt tired. It was around three pm when she opened her eyes. She had had the most delicious deep sleep, and still had no wish to paint. Had her desire to paint done? But perhaps not. Perhaps she was becoming refreshed and with new energies. moving to a new level of herself where the old got thrown out and new things took their place.

But, for the moment, she wanted to concentrate on an early supper…young new potatoes with butter and mint, and a casserole of feta cheese and spinach and perhaps some spring rolls with a crème Brule for dessert.

Then she caught sight of the dining-room table. That would be so much better than the breakfast bar, which was fine for a rushed breakfast. She found some place mats and set the table with a small bowl of fruit as a centre piece. It looked very inviting with the two wine glasses and the cutlery in place.

Of course, it was much too early for supper, but perhaps some snacks outside would be nice. Ivor may need to unwind. So she set up another small table with some snacks. Tea or coffee might be good, so she put out two cups and boiled the kettle.

It was a bit after half-past four when she heard Ivor's footsteps. She listened to them. Would they tell her how he was feeling? How the day went? She held her breath as she thought of Maureen, but was ready with a smile on her face when Ivor turned the corner and arrived at the front door.

He let out a big sigh of relief. "Seeing you brings back a sense of normality to life," he said.

Vivienne greeted him affably. "So how was your day?"

"Let me put down my briefcase and I'll unwind better," he said. "But I see you have set out some snacks to nibble on. That's a good idea."

"Would you like coffee or tea?" she asked. "The kettle has just boiled."

"Coffee, thanks, Vivienne," said Ivor.

While he went to his room to deposit his briefcase, Vivienne made the coffee and soon had two steaming cups to take to the outside table. She glanced at the distant view as she put down the two cups. Far off a blue sea with white waves was the focal point. The wild flowers and rocks and heathers that led down towards it was a perfect foil.

Soon Ivor was back with a great big sigh. Vivienne looked at him, but said nothing.

"That's the perfect way to converse with me, Vivienne," said Ivor, relaxing even more. "Let me unwind and then you can ask me how the day went."

Vivienne smiled. "How did it go?" she asked.

Ivor looked at her and his face relaxed as he said, "Perfectly. I took control of them immediately. They were there to learn watercolour painting, I was there to teach them about it, and any conversation was to be strictly kept to the course and what they were learning. They could chat at breaks or lunch. And I saw that I was fully occupied with students with questions at tea break and at lunch, I slipped out after I had eaten, to be away from talking and noise."

And to keep Maureen at bay! Vivienne thought. She didn't ask about Maureen and Ivor didn't talk about her. Ivor sat down and put biscuits and cheese squares onto a plate.

"Thanks for all of this, Vivienne. It's a perfect end to an excellent day of teaching." He smiled at her. "The walk at lunch time outside in amongst the heathers was perfect to clear my mind for the afternoon session."

Vivienne was curious to know what he had taught the students.

"I did it a bit differently from how I taught you. With them, I started at the beginning. With you, I started in the middle and you did very well. So today's lesson was just about learning to use the hake. I must say most of them were shocked at the size of it. But I started them off just with burnt sienna and the hake. I showed them how you can make long strokes with little sparkles in them, and long smooth strokes to create washes, which they will do tomorrow. And then I showed them how to hold the hake, so they could paint slender branches with the tip or strong main branches. If you use just the tip, you can outline houses and with the very tip, paint in small impressions of windows and doors. There is so much one can do with the hake, but practice is needed. And that is what they did today. Practice with the hake. Some were quite good by the end of today. Particularly, the two men."

Vivienne looked at Ivor questioningly. He seemed to know what she was thinking, because he put his arm around her shoulders and laughed a little. "No, I didn't give Maureen a chance to speak to me. I'll not put her off forever but, for today, I was safe."

"Are you worried about her?" asked Vivienne.

"I'm just concerned she may disrupt my serious artists. They have come to the course to learn, so control of the situation is my priority. But for now, let me enjoy this coffee and ask you how your day went?"

Vivienne put down her coffee cup. "You were quite right when you said to just do as the spirit moved me. For some strange reason I didn't want to paint today."

"So you slept?"

"No." Vivienne laughed. "Well, I did later on, but to start with I just felt I needed to do nothing, to walk amongst the wildflowers and rocks. Which is what I did... and then," she said, with a mysterious look on her face, "I met up with a rock that seemed like a very old man, and I just sat, getting to know that rock."

"That, Vivienne, is the perfect thing for an artist to do," said Ivor, with delight. "It is so hard to tell beginners like our students today that good art comes when one is not thinking. Just letting the silence enter the mind. That silent no-thought head is the artist's best friend. It is when the artist starts to think, to concentrate on drawing what he sees, that he or she misses the point. It is painting or drawing what you don't see that makes for good art. So how did you get on with your rock friend?"

"I sat for ages," said Vivienne, "then I remembered in one of my art books the method was to look for five minutes at something that takes your fancy, just look at it so that every detail is etched into one's mind. Then to close one's eyes for five minutes, then open them and without looking at what one is drawing, to look at the object and just sense it. and to draw what one feels or senses... I had a wonderful mystical time, even saw some coloured geometric shapes in the sky that didn't last for long, and then I looked at what I had drawn ... it was nothing like the old man in the rock, but it has a strange artistic quality about it ... I'll show you." She fished in her bag for her sketch book.

Ivor studied it and shook his head. "Wonderful, Vivienne, you did a perfect thing on your first day. Filled yourself with new energies. When you feel like painting, you will do so."

After that they chatted easily about what they were about to eat and what Ivor would teach the students tomorrow.

"More big brush but, this time, they'll learn how to do washes and how to create a landscape as you did, Vivienne."

Vivienne was suddenly glad she was not a student, repeating what she had learnt, but a free spirit investigating the energies of rocks and the earth.

"When would you like to eat, Ivor? It's simple fare tonight."

"Now would be perfect," said Ivor.

They waited until Vivienne had put the big dish of new potatoes with butter and mint and the large feta cheese and spinach casserole on the table. There was whole-wheat bread, as well, and soon both were enjoying their evening meal, whilst outside the sky darkened and the stars sparkled.

Supper over, and the table cleared of food and dishes. Ivor said, "I'm not a television fan. I'd like to put on my thinking jacket and sit outside where it will be such a pleasure to be without the glare of street lights." By now the gentle mantle of night was upon them. And Vivienne knew that this is what she wanted to do . Sit in the dark and tune in to the night.

So Vivienne sat in the dark with the far-off sight of the sea as it splashed a luminous white against the dark rocks in the light of the moon. Vivienne gave a huge sigh of satisfaction. Sitting in the dark on a comfortable chair with a warm blanket to keep out the chill she was just alone with herself, even though she was sitting beside a silent Ivor. Alone and listening … to the silence first and then strangely the small distinct night noises sounded a lot louder. Almost musical if it came to that. She sat eyes closed, listening. There was a great peace and silence in herself that she was aware of…that felt good, too, and she smiled in the dark. Still with her eyes closed, she was faintly aware of the body warmth of Ivor as he too sat soaking up the silence.

She wanted to giggle. What a way to spend time with a friend. Just sitting in the dark and saying and doing nothing. Well, was it nothing …? Vivienne had a feeling to open her eyes and what she saw was the firmament above, dark and alight with a million pin pricks of light. Now she sat looking skywards, aware of the dark, then strangely her night vision kicked in and the scene around her was as clear as day. Well, not quite, but close enough to see trees and shadows and little bushes, and the glowing eyes of was it a baboon peering out from behind a rock. Surely, they should all be asleep by now, thought Vivienne. She became aware that Ivor was sitting next to her.

She could clearly see the big warm wrap that he wore and she saw the way he had his head tilted backwards with his hair just touching his coat collar ... She could see that in her newfound night vision. Funny how, suddenly, it was if someone was shining a flashlight to show up the details of the land around. She turned her head and could clearly see the mountain looming up in the dark. And the path up to the Convention Centre, along with the twisty path that led between the rocks... she thought of the old man in the rocks she had seen only this morning and she was suddenly aware that she needed to watch her thoughts.

So she closed her eyes and sat again, watching what was going on in her mind. She was aware of a sudden desire to paint and she knew that tomorrow the paints would come out. She sighed and started as Ivor spoke in the darkness.

"We've both been silent for ages," he said. "I've had a marvellous time listening to night noises and getting everything else out of my head. And you, Vivienne?"

"Yes, I was listening, as well, though I did open my eyes a while ago to stare at the stars in the sky above. When I first looked the sky was very dark and the starry lights so beautiful, but then a strange thing happened. My night vision kicked in and it was no longer dark." She laughed. "It was like having a torch shine up in the sky. And the landscape was so clear... even in the distance. The sea and rocks were faintly visible."

Ivor said, "Quite an experience. Better than the TV, don't you think?"

Vivienne had to agree, but added, "But right now, I'm a bit stiff and a bit chilly. What do you say to a cup of hot chocolate indoors?"

She saw Ivor stand up and knew he was agreeable, so she too stood up and turned to go indoors. The light switch was easy to find and soon they were out of the magic of the night, back into a fairly normal night when Vivienne very soon had two mugs of hot chocolate and some biscuits organized. They sat comfortably, letting the silence they had both experienced fill them with a certain peace. It wasn't long after enjoying the hot chocolate and biscuits that Ivor turned gravely to Vivienne and gently squeezed her hand.

"I'll say goodnight now, Vivienne," he said. "I'll be up early to get a good day's lecturing done."

Vivienne said, "Thank you, Ivor, for inviting me. This is a magical time for me."

And it was. Her night's sleep was peaceful and she awoke to hear a very distant cock crowing to greet a new morning.

Was there a sunrise here and where? Unfortunately, she went back for just a few more minutes under the feathery duvet, but fell asleep and when she awoke, Mr Sun was shining cheerfully and she had missed the dawn.

She was soon up, showered , dressed and in the kitchen to make the coffee and a healthy cooked breakfast which was full and flavoursome. Ivor came through from his room showered and dressed and ready for the day. Vivienne watched as Ivor ate. He was clearly enjoying the fare. He lifted his bearded head when he saw her looking at him.

"I'm so glad you are here, Vivienne," he said, after swallowing a mouthful of food. "I would never be eating like this and it's good to start a day of teaching on a full stomach." He smiled at her before getting back to his food.

Vivienne was pleased. This was her role, that of caregiver and she watched as he completed his breakfast, finished his coffee, put down his paper napkin, nodded to her then stood up.

"Nice time to take a gentle stroll up there," he said. "And by the way,

I did have Maureen at me yesterday. I forgot all about her in the delight of last night's beauty."

"Oh," said Vivienne, trying not to sound too curious. "And what did she say?"

"Just that she wants time alone with me as she has a lot to say," he said, the smile going from his face. "It seems she has some deep dark secret about me that I have completely forgotten. I have no memory of Maureen at all."

"She said you were neighbours?"

"I can't even remember that," said Ivor, "and for now I don't want to think about it as I want to be fresh and precise today in how we approach our next lesson in watercolours, so let me keep my mind on my reason for being here. To teach them to paint...," he smiled, "with the big brush."

With another nod of his head, he walked to his room to collect his coat, his brief case of paints and papers, and he again nodded to Vivienne as he went out through the door. Vivienne stood watching him as he walked with strong determined steps, up the path leading towards the Convention Centre. In the wind, his shoulder-length light brown hair shone with a golden light and she wished him well. That he had a good painting day and, mentally, that he didn't have too hard a time with Maureen. Though she had to admit to herself that she was eager to hear what Maureen wanted him to know.

Vivienne took a long look at the day outside, at the sun shining on a distant gleaming sea, of the greenery around her with banks of small pretty wild flowers painting the picture for her. The ancient rocks that seemed everywhere just added to the rural charm.

An hour inside the cottage, had the breakfast cleared away and supper dealt with. Fried fish with a leafy green salad and she settled again for young new potatoes boiled and served with butter and mint along with some whole wheat bread and some varied cheese to eat with it. And an apple tart with cream as a dessert. For lunch she would have cheese and biscuits. And there was fruit juice and coffee. She took a deep breath.

Somewhere inside her was a tingling. A desire to get going with watercolours and paper ... a different feeling from the one she had had yesterday... yesterday had asked her to be still and she had taken it to mean just walk about and do nothing.

Today, her energy clearly wanted her to paint.

Just a short walk first, she thought and smiled as she thought of Ivor wanting to clear his head before painting. It was maybe such a feeling. So she laid her paper and paints ready on the dining-room table, along with water for washing her brush and for painting. She went outside and closed the front door .... Smiling, she remembered Lady Lavender telling her to be aware and to be in the moment. So she would walk and not think, just watch what she was doing, and where she was going , and what was around her... and, she decided, to watch what was inside herself as well. A slow wander started just outside the cottage, but grew in area as her feet felt the earth beneath them, a solid feeling of earthing herself. Making roots grow down into the earth, she thought, as she idly walked.

Yes, I am connected to all that is, she found herself thinking. She was intently looking at the small succulent green leaves and the firm prickly ones of the heathers…and observing the lovely hues of small purple flowers peeping out of a crevice. Intent only on her walk, Vivienne circled the cottage being also aware of the strange reddish mountain that loomed above them. Then she was back at the front door of the cottage.

She gave a big contented sigh. Nothing was in her head, nothing at all. She was ready to see what the paints produced for her that day. She would be like Ivor, put out the colours and let her brush decide which colours to use and what to do with them.

So the puddling with paint began and many hours passed with Vivienne in a dreamland of paints and paper. Her palette had large blobs of half a dozen colours … minus green, she knew how to mix it on the paper. And her brush was starting to work independently of her.

The food taken care of she had the day to herself. Vivienne had fortuitously put on her alarm for 3 pm and was startled when it rang. She was in the middle of a misty day on the mountains and wondered if she dare finish it, or if she needed to listen to the alarm and attend to the food. Just ten more minutes of painting and she was sure she could catch up with dinner as she usually left plenty of time. The ten minutes went quickly, but she was glad she had taken the chance as she had painted a lovely misty valley between towering mighty mountains. She washed her brush and wiped it dry, lying it lovingly on her palette. Now to shift her mind to another dimension, time to get supper ready.

She made up for lost time and soon had a small pot boiling with new potatoes, a green salad in a bowl and fish frying on the hotplate. With whole wheat bread, it would be a tasty meal and, clearly, so thought Ivor, as he came in, smiling.

"I smelled that fish and knew what we were eating," he said, as he carefully placed his briefcase on the floor. His eyes flew to Vivienne's painting of mountains. Ivor stood, looking at it, whilst Vivienne waited, her breath held.

From the painting Ivor lifted his eyes to Vivienne's. "You have caught the mist in the mountains, Vivienne," he said. "That's advanced work and it's great you are mastering so many techniques."

Vivienne let out her breath. "Whew," she said, "it matters to me that you like it."

Ivor had walked over to where she stood at the kitchen bar counter.

"It shouldn't matter, Vivienne. You paint now because it's in your soul, so you paint for you, not for my approval." He said it kindly and Vivienne smiled.

"Thanks, Ivor, but you are my teacher ..."

"You are past the teacher stage, Vivienne," said Ivor. "You are a creative watercolour artist now. Painting is what matters to you." He turned to say, "That food makes me feel so hungry, Vivienne.... Is it ready?"

"Oh yes," said Vivienne, "let's just take the plates of food and the salad and bread over to the table, which I've cleared of my painting materials....except for the watercolour of the mountains. I wasn't ready to pack that one away, so it will share the dining-room table with us."

"Artists do things differently," said Ivor, pulling out a chair, ready for a piece of whole-wheat bread, which he buttered.

"That fish smells wonderful," he said, "so thank you, Vivienne. I'm starting to eat." Soon, both were engaged in eating and conversation had stopped. Vivienne had custard and fruit salad as desert, instead of the apple pie and cream she had planned. While they were enjoying it, Ivor spoke about his day.

"It was very successful, Vivienne. I had them all painting delightful scenes all in shades of burnt umber. But they learnt the value of dark areas and light areas and they are ready now for tomorrow when we branch into colour."

Vivienne was wanting to ask questions about Maureen, but Ivor volunteered information on his own.

"Maureen got me alone," he said. "I did not enjoy the time at all. It seems she has her eye on me as a prospective husband." He gave a choking laugh at this, "and has been harbouring that idea since she was seventeen years old. I still don't remember any of it at all, but she assures me she helped me what she calls 'escape' my disastrous family. And it seems she meant to follow me and to tie me to her ..."

He gave a slight shudder and Vivienne was appalled. *What was she hearing?*

"But, Ivor, did you intend to marry her?" she managed to gasp out.

Ivor shook his head. "Vivienne, I have no memory at all of her and very little of my parents. It wasn't an easy adolescence. I do remember that, but seem to have blotted it out of my memory. All of this was a very long time ago."

"But marriage, Ivor.... You've never spoken about marriage... Not in the six months I have known you."

"Because, a long time ago, I decided it was not for me. I am an artist, married to my paints and brushes and what they produce. And I enjoy teaching. Those satisfy my soul. Marriage has never entered my mind."

"But Maureen seems to think differently," persisted Vivienne.

"Yes, she does, and it is not pleasant, Vivienne. Not at all. I don't like the woman, but treat her no differently from the other students. In class, she behaves because that is the standard I have set, but she caught me in the lunch break. I thought I had dodged her, but she was too clever for me and was waiting on the path outside the back of the Centre.

"Remember, Ivor, darling," she said, "you were to get engaged to me. We were both seventeen and I helped you to get away from your father.

You depended on me."

"I told her I could recall none of it, but she persisted and tried to etch in details, so I might remember. She wore a red sundress, she said, because she used to have one that I liked. She thought it would jolt my memory. And I wore terrible old clothes that she wanted me to ditch and dress properly. I can't remember anything, Vivienne, which is very disturbing."

"Did she say where you lived?" asked Vivienne.

"Yes, she described an old house next door to her new council house. It is all so far back in my memory that I don't remember. I know I lived in the city centre and didn't like it at all. And I remember the argument I had when I was fourteen with the art teacher, who said clouds had to be white and the sky blue. I remember tossing down my brush and walking out ...It's all very vague, but I, much later on, after this period that I can't remember, found a great artist who taught me about colour and let me paint red clouds." He laughed at this and touched Vivienne lightly on the arm.

"I don't like talking about this, Vivienne, so, do you mind if we drop the subject? I'll do my best to avoid Maureen, but it won't be that easy. She joined this class simply to track me down."

"Okay," said Vivienne, "so shall we clear up and you can tell me what you intend painting tomorrow?"

Soon after, comfortably seated in the lounge with the late-afternoon sun touching the landscape, they sat in two easy chairs.

"It's always so great to show students how to mix colours so that they get the shades and colours they want," he said with excitement in his voice. "Beginners often buy too many tubes of paint. Green for instance. They love tubes of quite violent green. It is so lovely to show them how three tubes of paint can produce the softest new growth greens and the deepest evergreens ... and it is often done on the paper itself.

"So I will be showing them a lot of colour mixing. Then possibly we will paint skies. You have a love of the dawn. I have a love of skies in general. At all times of the day. And in all kinds of weather. That is why students learn to use Payne's grey and alizarin crimson in their clouds."

Vivienne was listening. She hadn't really tried too hard with clouds. But this was inspiring her. Maybe tomorrow she would see what she could do with sunsets and dull dark days...with just that small glimmer of light shining through. She looked at Ivor and smiled.

"You do inspire," she said, "I'm already thinking of painting clouds myself tomorrow."

"That's good to hear," said Ivor. "But I'll also show them how to paint leaves on trees. They are all different, have different shapes and different shades of green and, of course, there is the sunlight and shadows to take into account. So they won't get any scenes painted. Just a lot of practice." He smiled at Vivienne and she saw that crinkly smile of his that somehow disappeared into his beard. He looked happy.

She was glad, because she was happy just sitting here listening to him. Then Ivor stood up.

"Vivienne, I need to take a stroll outside, in the early evening … again to empty my head and just absorb the energies that are here. Do you mind?"

She shook her head. "Of course not, Ivor, that's fine." she said, but inwardly she wanted to say she would love to join him. But something stopped her. She felt he needed to be alone, to be quiet, to come to terms with Maureen, and to be ready for his exciting day tomorrow. She would sit inside and do nothing. Wasn't that what Lady Lavender had taught her to do?

So, whilst Ivor walked outside for half an hour, Vivienne sat on the couch looking out towards the ocean, which she could just glimpse in the late-afternoon half-light. Her mind wanted suddenly to jump to Steven, but she brought it back to the room and the moment. To being in a new environment...she stood up. Some hot chocolate with some marsh-mallows might be welcome when Ivor came inside. It was chilly outside.

There were also the supper dishes to wash up and the kitchen to tidy all of which kept her in the moment. So when a refreshed Ivor returned, he was pleased with the hot chocolate and laughed at the marshmallows.

"I haven't had marshmallows ever, I think," said Ivor. "They froth up, don't they?"

"That's the idea," said Vivienne, as they both sat down with soft marshmallows topping their hot chocolate.

"I'm loving this course," said Ivor, "and had a good walk outside. If you don't mind, I'll turn in shortly."

"Not at all," said Vivienne. "Then I'll see you at breakfast in the morning."

True to her word, Vivienne showered, and had a tasty hot breakfast ready first thing in the morning. Ivor was thoughtful as he ate, and Vivienne didn't like to interrupt that mood. It wasn't a heavy mood, just one that seemed to ask her not to talk, so she did not.

After he had eaten, Ivor smiled at Vivienne. "You are the best," he said. "That was perfect to start to what might be a difficult day." He nodded to her as he picked up his briefcase and jacket and soon was walking up the path to the Convention Centre.

Vivienne's day was much the same as yesterday. She thought ahead about supper, a frozen quiche of cheese seemed a good idea with salad .. after that she had a walk outside, longer than before and one that took her past her old-man rock and past the heathers and small bright flowers. It filled her with a sense of delight and she was happy to spend the rest of the day experimenting with clouds. Again her alarm told her when it was time to put the quiche in the oven and to prepare a salad and clear off her painting materials.

She heard the footsteps and by the sound of them she could tell he was in some kind of a perturbed state of mind. She just knew the different sounds of his footsteps and these were not those of a peaceful man.

True enough, he entered, pulling at his hair.

Vivienne looked at him in alarm.

"Yes, Vivienne, it is every bit as bad as that," he said, putting down his briefcase and slumping into a chair. Vivienne said nothing, but waited for him to explain.

"No, not the painting, but that awful woman... Maureen."

Vivienne watched as he pulled at his hair, and shook his head, his eyes downcast. Vivienne said nothing. He was obviously deeply disturbed.

Ivor continued, now looking at Vivienne. "Vivienne, ever since I was a young man, I have never thought of getting married. My life partner was my art. My love of paints, colour, light and painting. This Maureen has shaken me terribly."

He paused. Vivienne still said nothing, but looked at him, her eyes showing her support. Ivor took a deep breath and continued. "I have kept much to myself, have never spoken to anyone, but Maureen has dug up a past I have no memory of. No memory of being seventeen when she was seventeen. No memory of her reporting to my father that I was painting when he had forbidden it. No memory of the thrashing he gave me. No memory of her helping me to escape and find foster care." He stopped and his hazel eyes, usually so full of light, were sombre.

"She insists she proposed to me, not me to her. My reward to her for getting me foster care was that I was to marry her when we were both eighteen. But I escaped the foster care, which I do not recall and I just remember a brilliant time in my life when I was apprenticed to a wonderful creative artist, Gem Huckleberry, a former alcoholic, who strictly avoided any social functions and lived solely for his art. He had studied astronomy, electricity and much more in getting to understand light. You get colour by killing colour, he told me.

"So I helped him all I could and, in return, he fed me and taught me much that is my basis for art, which is my living. In the East, they call it *chi* ... the life force in each

63

person or animal. The light force that shines in the eyes of a person or animal. And it is this life force that inhabits us all. We breathe, we live..."

He stopped for breath. Vivienne was learning new things about art and about Ivor. She remembered her lesson with Lady Lavender to MYOB. She did not ask questions. She let Ivor lean back and sigh then breathe deeply. He seemed to be getting back to the Ivor she had got to know.

He continued, "I really do not know what to do, Vivienne, to stop her advances."

Vivienne had a sudden flash of an idea, but it seemed too brazen to air. Surprisingly, however, Ivor came up with the same idea.

"I've just thought, Vivienne, you could help me by agreeing with me that just for this workshop that I let it slip that you are more than a friend."

He smiled at her. The old Ivor was back. "Maybe I tell them you are my partner, not only in art, but in a relationship." He laughed and touched Vivienne's arm. "Would you go along with that, Vivienne?"

Vivienne noticed that he didn't say that he and Vivienne were to marry, just that they had a personal relationship.

Vivienne smiled at him. "Of course, that's fine, Ivor," she said. "I'm truly honoured."

It was obviously too painful a subject for him. She squeezed his arm. "Ivor, we've been close friends for six months now, so this is a natural progression," she said.

Ivor chuckled. "Next time, Maureen tries this 'engaged to you' stunt, I have an answer. Now I smell some delicious savoury food. When do we eat? I'm actually starving."

With the food, the atmosphere changed. No longer was Maureen a cloud over them. There was just Ivor and Vivienne, enjoying the food and their simple relationship.

Chapter 4

That evening the savoury tart had mushrooms, bacon and cheese as a filling. Vivienne watched as Ivor ate with obvious enjoyment.

"I really look forward to the end of my day," he said, "because I know what tasty food you will have prepared, and it was my genius in asking you to come along."

He smiled at Vivienne. She also had some good brie cheeses and biscuits, and a glass of wine. Her dessert this evening was something quite different. Rhubarb pie and custard.

"I haven't eaten rhubarb for a very long time," said Ivor. "Again, you have genius on your side when it comes to food."

The tasty food, the glass of well-chilled wine, and an early soft dusk as night settled in made for a comfortable end to the day. Ivor again went for his customary walk, and Vivienne washed and tidied. She hadn't shown him her efforts today at clouds. She was finding it interesting the way the paints settled themselves into cloudy skies with different lighting. And she was loving the relationship she was developing with paints and paper.

At the end of the day, just before he retired, Ivor asked to see what she had painted and she put down her five sheets of watercolour paper, all with different skies and different lighting. She had painted a late-afternoon sunset sky with reds and golds, a rainy day with impending storm... the clouds were tinged with alizarin crimson and Payne's grey and she had got some lovely lights shining through the darkness. Vivienne was pleased with what she had done and felt good when Ivor studied them then looked at her and smiled.

"You pick up what to do so easily, Vivienne...just by listening to me you have absorbed the way to get interesting skies. Remember that if you have a very busy and interesting sky you need just a simple foreground. Also, the relation between the area for sky and for land depends on what is predominant. If it is the sky then you use more than half, perhaps three quarters of the paper for the sky and the foreground is simple and takes up the final quarter. Conversely, if it is the foreground that your picture is about, then the sky is much less than a half a page." He nodded and smiled, as if sure that Vivienne understood.

Vivienne did. "And tomorrow what are your students painting? You are almost half way through your week, Ivor."

"I know and by the end of the week I am confident they will all be able to paint attractive creative watercolours." Ivor seemed relaxed and happy.

In that frame of mind, he took himself to bed, ... leaving Vivienne alone to spend some time outside in her easy chair just doing nothing, but enjoying the myriad of stars in a dark sky. Tonight, her night vision did not kick in so the scene remained dark with a sprinkling of brilliant shining stars in the vast expanse of the sky.

The next day, began in a similar fashion. Vivienne was glad she was sleeping soundly and peacefully. She varied her breakfasts, which were always substantial to give Ivor a good foundation for his day. He was cheerful as he ate breakfast, picked up his bag, gave her a friendly pat on the arm, smiled at her and trudged out of the cottage and up to the Convention Centre. Vivienne knew to keep her mind off wondering how he was coping and to simply stay in the moment, get the cottage tidy, clear up after breakfast and get another tasty supper ready.

Today, she decided to sit outside on a chair beside a large rock that would do as a painting table and just to paint what she saw…small rocky outcrops, green leaves of heathers and other plants and a myriad of small brightly coloured wild flowers that peeped out from unexpected places. Vivienne spent a great deal of time in just looking at the plants, and the distant shining surf, and at the sky, a simple pale-blue with some wispy white clouds. A small wild animal ran across the path. Was it a rock rabbit? She wasn't sure and a baboon barked a greeting.

Vivienne's heart was full with the joy of just being there among the flowers, the rocks and the birds and wild animals and she was in no hurry today to paint. It seemed to be a day that said she was to take things slowly, to absorb what was around her and not to rush to paints and paper.

Listen to my body, listen to my intuition, she said in her mind. No, I'm not being lazy, I'm absorbing new energies that are here in these rocks and plants. So she packed away her paints ... and her sketch book... and determined just to rest. Think nothing, look and listen. Listen to what she didn't know, but she knew suddenly that it was an inner listening ... she was learning to go within and to become one with her own spirit, as well as the spirit of all that was around her. It was joyous and humbling. And Vivienne felt renewed. How could a simple 'do nothing' result in this feeling of peace. For one very brief moment her mind slipped over to Maureen and Ivor, but she quickly pulled it back...back to the moment when the warming sun shone down on her.

Vivienne dozed in the sunshine. She woke with a surprise to find it was well past lunch time. She went back to the cottage for a snack. A few small birds were there, hoping for some crumbs, so she shared her bread roll and crackers with the birds ... They brought their friends and Vivienne was entertained to a dozen or more birds, all at her door, busily eating bits of bread and biscuits.

How hard would it be to paint a bird? she wondered. She remembered the Chinese way was to start with the eyes, with the light in the eyes, and go from there.

A sudden desire to use her sketch book brought her to action. Leave out what doesn't interest you, she remembered. And start with the eyes. And remember the white spaces are part of the picture.

One little bird seemed to know she needed a model, so it obligingly sat still, side-on to her, whilst she quickly drew the eye, leaving a small speck of nothingness that was the *chi*, or light, then the top of the head and the beak... a couple of short swift stokes showed where the body and back were, and a few quick strokes gave the indication of a feathery wing.... Now two little spindly legs...Vivienne smiled in delight. She had captured a bird's spirit, and a bird, indeed, on her paper. She couldn't wait to show Ivor...She had dinner to prepare, but Ivor had sent her a message: *Don't prepare dinner, we are eating at the restaurant tonight....* and then Ivor would come to fetch her. She was quiet as she wondered how his day had been.

She heard his footsteps and today they were different. Almost triumphant. She smiled to herself and went outside to greet Ivor who smiled at her, put down his briefcase and gave her a hug. This surprised Vivienne. What was so good that Ivor was behaving in this relaxed and joyous mood?

"Please don't worry to change, Vivienne, but please get your jacket and come with me to the Convention Centre. This is important."

Vivienne didn't argue. She got her jacket and they exited the cottage and walked up the hill towards the Convention Centre. Ivor surprised Vivienne by taking her arm in his and drawing her close to him. Was this to show Maureen there was a bond between them? She didn't know, but it did feel comforting to be walking closely with Ivor. He didn't speak as they walked, but there was a cheery spirit she could sense...

As they neared the Centre, Ivor said, "Maureen will be waiting for us so just act naturally." This was alarming to Vivienne. She wasn't sure she wanted to meet Maureen whilst attached, as she was, to Ivor.

But Ivor seemed confident that this was the right way to deal with the situation.

As they entered the foyer of the reception room, Maureen, in a tight fitting gunmetal grey shiny dress, her dark hair hanging over her shoulders and her dark eyes glinting, was waiting for them.

"Now let's sit down, shall we?" said Ivor, "so we can talk this out comfortably." And he pointed to a corner table with three large comfy chairs.

"That would be the best thing to do, wouldn't it, my love?" Maureen gave his hair a playful ruffle. She walked ahead with a model's hip-swinging gait. Vivienne noticed that Ivor's eyes were glued on her.

Vivienne's heart was pounding. This was not a situation she had prepared herself for and, by the look on Ivor's face, nor was it one he had expected.

"Vivienne and I are booked in the dining room for dinner, but we can have starters and a drink here, and talk this out, Maureen. Now Maureen, please don't talk until we have ordered and have something to drink and eat in front of us."

Maureen was breathing heavily, obviously working at getting some control over rampant feelings. Ivor squeezed Vivienne's hand tightly and she was glad of his strength. What made it worse was that Maureen completely ignored Vivienne's presence, as if she didn't exist, honing solely into "her man". It made Vivienne feel helpless and inadequate. And not having changed for dinner made her feel worse.

The waiter appeared.

"A double brandy for me," said Maureen defiantly, staring soulfully at Ivor. "Do you remember that's what we both used to drink?"

Ivor made a hand gesture requiring her to stop speaking.

"This needs to wait, Maureen," he said sternly. "We are ordering, please." He turned to Vivienne. "What would you like to drink?"

"A sweet rosé please," said Vivienne, thankful that Maureen was silent.

"And I'll have a glass of dry red wine, and to eat? Starters to begin with. You, Maureen?" He deliberately was challenging her to behave properly.

"Snails peri peri," said Maureen, with a small amused smile.

The witch knew she had rattled them both, thought Vivienne.

"And I'll have creamed mushrooms," said Vivienne.

"And make it prawns for me," said Ivor. As the waiter went off, he silenced Maureen.

"Maureen, we will wait until our drinks and starters arrive before you start."

Vivienne noticed that he did have some power over Maureen as she was silent, but wore the same amused look on her face. Vivienne shivered slightly.

"Are you cold?" asked Ivor in concern.

"Not really," said Vivienne, but Ivor put his arm around her and drew her closer.

"There is a chill in the night air," he said.

The waiter reappeared with their drinks, indicating that their starters would be along shortly.

"Right," said Ivor, "then I would formally like to introduce my most revered partner, Vivienne, to you, Maureen. I have made a commitment to Vivienne, by which I stand."

The starters had arrived and Maureen drew in a sultry breath whilst the waiter put them in the correct places.

"You, Ivor, my darling, don't you understand, are already betrothed to me, so any relationship you may have formed since, is simply not valid. I have waited a very long time, but I knew you would not marry, I have kept my eye on you," she said. "It has been hard, but every so often you appeared in the news at some art exhibition and, this time, I was able to contact you in person." She gave Ivor a sexy smile, and draped her fingers along his arm. Ivor recoiled slightly and shook his head.

"Don't shake your head, Ivor," she said. "We might have only been seventeen years of age, but we knew what we wanted. We still do. Else you would have married years ago. Face it, you were waiting for me."

Ivor shook his head again. "Don't pretend you don't remember, Ivor, my love," said Maureen, in a soothing tone.

"Maureen, my partner and I are in a restaurant for a meal," commanded Ivor. "Please respect this."

"No, I won't," said Maureen her voice rising, her veneer slipping slightly. "You ducked away from the friends of mine who were providing you with food and shelter. Tut, tut. just took off... a bit rude, don't you think? You didn't even let me know where you were going. I had no idea where you had gone. But I caught up with you years later when I read in a newspaper that you were exhibiting pictures in Spain. Of course, I couldn't get to Spain, but I started putting cuttings into a file." She pulled out of her bag a big shabby folder with many newspaper cuttings it. "All about you, Ivor. I haven't waited all these years to be side-tracked by *anyone.*"

Ivor drew Vivienne closer to him, but Maureen acted as if Vivienne didn't exist.

Very quietly Ivor said to Vivienne, "Don't say anything. Don't get into an argument. It will prove nothing."

With her voice rising Maureen said, "You are not getting out of this, Ivor. A man commits to one woman then take up with another. Oh no. I have first claim on him. I have waited all these long years and our betrothal is still as clear to me now as it was when we were seventeen. How would I know your name and know of your passion for painting ... you were painting abstract stuff ... a bit crazy, but you were crazy then. You *must* remember..." She was angry now.

Vivienne felt this was all like a bad dream.

"And I am not letting you go, baby," said Maureen, angrily digging into her plate of snails.

Vivienne was breathing deeply and her face was flushed with emotion.

Ivor was saying nothing, but looking at Maureen with a steady gaze.

"Now, Maureen, you have had a chance to tell us both properly, without yelling. I can remember nothing of what you are talking about."

Despite the warning for her not to shout, Maureen raised her voice. "Ivor, when you were seventeen, you were my neighbour. You lived in a tumbledown old house with your vicious father. He was a boxer and wanted you to be one, too, but you had chosen to be an artist. *Can't you remember?"* She stared at Ivor with a slight frown wrinkling her forehead.

"Nothing at all," said Ivor. *"Nothing."*

"I taught you to drink double brandies so that your father wouldn't get to you so badly. And I knew he had forbidden you to paint and, yes, I told him you were still painting. And yes, he thrashed you almost unconscious after that. *Don't you remember?* I got friends of mine with a car to fetch you and take you with them to give you food and shelter and I had said to you, deal was we would get married when we were both eighteen. Our birthdays are within days of each other... How would I know all this if you hadn't told me?"

Ivor shook his head. "I have no memory of it at all, Maureen. None."

"Well, I have all these cuttings proving I have been waiting to meet you again, but it has been very hard to find out where you were. Until I saw that exhibition in Simonstown and the course to take place after it. I knew I had to join it. And so I have. And I expect you to keep that early commitment."

Ivor was looking at her steadily. Vivienne's heart was racing.

"If I had to escape your caregivers, it doesn't sound to me like *I* was convinced of any early engagement to you, Maureen," he said.

"Poor darling, your words now are not going to loosen the hold I have on you. And you know why? Because you want me, too. I know you do."

With a nod to Ivor, she pushed back her chair stalked off.

Vivienne turned a distressed face towards Ivor. "I thought you said we were going to have a nice dinner," she said.

Ivor looked contrite. "Vivienne, I knew Maureen would be waiting for us, but I never in my life expected that she would be so disgusting."

"And she hasn't finished with you yet, she said," reminded Vivienne.

Ivor looked tense. "Vivienne there is no way I would ever consider her as a partner, and certainly not as a marriage partner, so please let us drop this for now...If you are ready let's go through to the dining room ..." He smiled slightly into his beard. "There's a new atmosphere there. And a nice menu to study." Vivienne stood up and so did Ivor. Then taking her gently by the arm, he led her through the double glass doors into the dining room. The atmosphere was, indeed, different, with candles on the tables and a soft fragrance.

Vivienne turned to Ivor and smiled. "Alright, Ivor, it's dinner and it's just you and me. Deal?"

He hugged her and smiled at her. "Yes, deal," he replied.

Vivienne was impressed with this new side of Ivor as he pulled out a chair for her and saw that she was

77

comfortably seated. The restaurant was not busy. It seated perhaps thirty people, but the tables were attractively set out with a rose in a vase and linen table napkins. Soft music was playing and Vivienne relaxed. She sighed deeply and looked at Ivor.

"I'm most terribly sorry for what you have just been through," he said. "She is a dreadful woman."

"But she must have known you when you were young."

"Yes, she has proved it, but I can't remember and her report of it is all as she saw it and how she saved me. I really don't want to talk about it, Vivienne. It's very distressing to me. What made it even more distressing is that I expected her to attack *you*, at any minute."

Vivienne shivered. "It's not nice, Ivor, but agreed. Let's leave Maureen out of this meal. What's the menu like?"

Both of them picked up menus at their places whilst a courteous waiter waited for their decisions.

"A chicken curry for me," said Ivor. "I love curries."

Vivienne remembered what her friend, Henriette, had said about curries in the Cape … so she chose a pineapple chicken dish. Both ordered a glass of wine and clinked them to wish each other success. Vivienne was relaxing with the pleasing ambience and Ivor's steady influence.

"I didn't see what you painted today, Vivienne," he said.

"I took the day off," said Vivienne. "Just enjoyed the silence and the energies and the natural surroundings. Until one little bird sat for a sitting, then I drew and briefly painted the bird. I was happy with it as I seemed to catch it's spirit."

"I love to hear you talk like this," said Ivor, bending forward and looking into Vivienne's eyes. "It's my great luck to have met someone who speaks my language... that of the creative artist... who sees art everywhere."

The food had arrived so both stopped talking and began the serious business of eating. Vivienne watched as Ivor took a forkful of curry. What would his reaction be? He was clearly delighted with it.

"Great curry," he said. "I'm glad I ordered it."

So much, thought Vivienne, for Henriette's advice on curries in the Cape. The rest of her advice was probably as suspect and she smiled.

"Why the smile, Vivienne?" asked Ivor.

"Oh, I'm just remembering a friend's remark about Kalk Bay and me coming here," she said. "She was wrong on the curry thing ... said they can't make curry here, and I was wondering what other points she had wrong."

Ivor nodded. "People's opinions are just that, opinions. We learn to make our own assessments."

"Oh, yes. and I remember she said it was windy here and how I didn't like the wind. But, Ivor, I've found I *do* like the wind, especially the wind in your open car."

Ivor smiled. "I'm glad you like my car, Vivienne ... we will make many more trips in it to places that are good to paint."

And so, the evening progressed with a delicious dessert and a cappuccino coffee to finish it off. By the time they reached the cottage, Maureen was forgotten...

"I'll have an early night if you don't mind, Vivienne. Tomorrow, we will be painting water. The breaking waves, the ripples in a river and many other water features. I need to be clear-headed and rested."

Vivienne watched as he disappeared into his bedroom. She wasn't ready to sleep. She knew she needed to likewise clear her head and it was best done wrapped in a blanket sitting outside in a chair and being quiet ... being aware of the vastness of the universe with its myriad shining stars. Such a privilege to be here and doing this would quiet her mildly troubled mind ...

Chapter 5

The next morning after his nicely cooked breakfast, Ivor gave Vivienne an unexpected hug.

"That's for good cheer for us both for today," he said. "I'll train on water and my best wishes are that you have a good day today, Vivienne." He looked her in the eye with a serious expression.

Vivienne stepped back and smiled at Ivor.

"That will make certain my day is good," she said, "and thank you, Ivor."

She watched as he slung his jacket over his shoulders, picked up his large case of painting materials and strode with strong determined steps up the path towards the Convention Centre. As he approached it, she saw him stop to greet a group of students. He's okay, she breathed to herself. He keeps good control of his class. It's me who doesn't feel so good. She had an uncomfortable niggle at the back of her mind. She knew it was to do with Maureen's strange possessive behaviour over Ivor. She was convinced that what the woman had said was basically true, but for her to expect a middle-aged man to honour a pledge that he had made at that tender age of seventeen was nothing short of bizarre. The woman was mentally unstable.

Vivienne turned her attention first to clearing up after breakfast and doing minimal house work. Then she decided not to paint, but to walk and just look. Staying silent and in the moment. In this frame of mind, she wandered in the large heather-covered grounds for a long time. She kept her mind firmly on the moment, smelling the fragrance of flowers and foliage and the earth. The sea looked tempting and though Ivor had said to wait for him on Saturday, she decided to walk down towards the rocky shore with the crashing waves. She knew the inner cleansing the combination of the sea and sand did and she, somehow, felt she needed that today. No, she wouldn't paint or sketch. She would make her way down to the large splashing waves and the bit of rocky beach and just relax.

It was a half an hour's walk through tricky rocks and heathers, but at last she was at the beach. There was a short stretch of beach sand with large rocks jutting out into a sea that splashed foaming breakers against them, sending up sprays of water that wet her skin.

Vivienne laughed. This was just what she needed. A way to entirely be in the present moment with nothing but the sea and sand in her head. A few sea gulls were searching for food in the pools of still water. Then from round the one rock came a figure. A figure in shimmering deep blue. Vivienne, jumped. What was it? ... Was it a *mermaid...*? Silly idea. No, it wasn't, but she needed the upliftment of fanciful notions. The ordeal of Maureen still sat with her.

A woman with long shining golden hair had appeared from behind a rock. She was wearing a tight-fitting, blue swimming costume with a shimmering long blue sarong tied around her waist. It made it look as if she had the body of a mermaid. Vivienne smiled... the woman caught her smile. And smiled back at her. Her eyes were a lovely shade of blue.

"Might I ask what pleases you so?" she asked.

"To tell you the truth, I thought you were a mermaid with your blue bathing suit and sarong," said Vivienne. "Silly me."

"Not so silly," said the woman. "This is Mermaid Beach and it has been said that a mermaid has been seen sitting on these very rocks."

The woman found a flat rock of a comfortable height and sat down on it. She smiled at Vivienne.

"You new to these parts?" she asked.

"Oh yes, I'm part of an artists' week-long course. Actually, I'm partner to the lecturer," she amended. "So I'm just exploring the area. We live up there." Turning, she indicated the cottages far up the hillside. "And you?" she questioned.

"I live here," said the woman. "My passion is photography...I have my own studio, but love the beach and the waves, so I spend a lot of my spare time here. I could show you my studio if you have the time."

Vivienne did have the time and today was not a day for painting.

"It's not that far away," said the woman. "By the way, my name is Julie."

"And I am Vivienne," said Vivienne. She liked this mermaid-like woman, and smiled. "Yes, I'd love to see your studio."

"My beach sandals are behind that rock. I'll put them on and I'm ready to take you there." Julie's shining golden hair befitted a mermaid, thought Vivienne, and those big blue eyes. From behind a rock, she produced a pair of blue-and-white beach sandals. "Right," she said, "follow me."

She led Vivienne through a small windy path in the heather to a circular building that had an outlook onto a small private road.

"People can find me if they are interested in photography," she said.

"I am fairly well known. I'm taking you in via the back entrance."

The building had large glass windows that had shutters that were open. It had a back entrance where she ushered Vivienne past an open tea garden, then past a small kitchen and small living areas that led into a large circular exhibition room filled with large framed photographs. Many were in black and white, emphasizing the back lighting and the drama of that particular scene.

Vivienne's eyes turned to a picture that drew her to it. It was of a few strands of flowering grass, standing tall with backlighting shining like a halo round the individual small seed heads, so simple and yet so riveting and so tranquil. One could live very peacefully with the simplicity and drama of such a picture. Julie was watching her, aware of her good reaction to the photograph of the grasses. She stood slightly behind Vivienne as she moved on to other pictures. Backlighting seemed to be Julie's favourite special effect.

"They are all so special," said Vivienne. "Clients must find it hard to decide which to buy."

Julie nodded in satisfaction. "I like it when they struggle," she said, "because I, myself, don't know which I like best. It all depends on the person and where he or she is going to hang the picture."

Vivienne must have spent an hour walking slowly around the gallery.

She was so glad of this interlude. And she said to Julie, "I may come back on Saturday with my partner." It felt right to say that and yet it made her feel nervous. "He is an artist and I'm sure he'd love to see your form of art."

"That's great." said Julie. "My shop is open from nine on Saturday until one. I'll be here … but for now would you like to sit in the tea garden with me and enjoy a cool drink or coffee… and a chat… I'd love to hear more about the art workshop. I do a bit of painting myself. One art form is often related to another."

Vivienne felt she had made a friend in Julie. And it was as if they had known each other for years as they fell into easy conversation. This was mostly about art and painting and photography, but at the same time each allowed the other a glimpse of her real person. Vivienne was so glad of this interlude. It gave her back her faith in humanity.

"Ivor also has a workshop for the group on Saturday afternoon," said Vivienne. "I think it is open to outside artists as well as he invited me to join in. Perhaps you might like to join us?"

"I'd love that," said Julie. "Strange how we met but I feel I've known you for years." And she smiled at Vivienne with her big blue eyes sparkling.

Vivienne smiled back. This was a joyous soul and so refreshing to her on this particular day. After the refreshments, Vivienne said goodbye to Julie, assuring her that she would easily find her way back to the beach and then up the hillside to their rented cottage without a problem. It was after two when Vivienne reached the cottage. Quite exhausted from all the walking she found a frozen savoury tart, which, with a salad would make an easy supper. Before getting the supper going, she wondered how Ivor's day had gone. She was feeling better after her visit to Julie's gallery, but still there was this nasty niggle in her head … she knew it had something to do with Maureen.

Her savoury tart was smelling good when Ivor returned. He smiled at Vivienne and she could tell by the way he looked at her that his day had been reasonable. No drama, she sensed. She hadn't had any drama either, but still had this nasty feeling. However, she didn't discuss it with Ivor, just told him about the mermaid behind the rock, at which he smiled, and then about the visit to a photographic studio. He was interested in this and agreed, on Saturday, they would visit it together.

It was his morning off the class and yes, he would drive Vivienne there going along the main road and then down the little private road that led to the studio. And yes, if she painted, Julie was welcome to join the afternoon session for the class students and others interested in painting. Ivor didn't mention Maureen and Vivienne didn't feel like bringing her into their lives again, so asked no questions about her. Their supper was pleasant with much the same procedure of Ivor walking outside by himself then them both chatting a while before Ivor took himself off to bed.

Friday followed much the same pattern, but, this time, Vivienne did brief sketches outside. She had temporarily lost interest in painting, but the love for it would come back, she was sure. Ivor returned happy that their last day had been a success. The class had all painted their own creative pictures that included all facets he had been training them on. Splashing sea, trees, clouds, water and hills and mountains. All were happy, he said, not mentioning Maureen... then he added that he had told them about the photographic studio if any would like to visit now that their art course was over.

Saturday dawned into a beautiful tranquil day and, after breakfast, Ivor and Vivienne locked up the cottage and both got into his blue open sports car. They drove slowly up the long road towards the road, and Vivienne noticed a car from one of the other cottages following behind them. This was of no consequence to her until she noticed in her rear-view mirror that the car was turning off the main road and taking the short private road to Julie's gallery. Strange, she thought.

Ivor drew his car into the visitors' parking area and got out, helped Vivienne out, left the car unlocked and walked with Vivienne towards the studio.

Vivienne was curious to know who was in the other car, but didn't look. It was only when they were in the studio, walking around looking at the framed photos, that she noticed that the other visitor was none other than Maureen.

Maureen. How did she know about the studio and what was she doing here? Of course, she remembered Ivor had told the students about the photographic studio so that explained Maureen's presence – for now, she was just walking around looking at the pictures. But Vivienne had a horrid feeling that this was not going to end well…

Two more cars had arrived and four more visitors were walking around. "I only open on weekends," said Julie, "so I do have a fair amount of traffic during the weekend."

Ivor was absorbed in gazing at the various backlit pictures. No one was talking, of which Vivienne was glad. She had seen all these pictures yesterday and wanted to make sure she kept out of Maureen's way. So, as soon as she could she slipped out of the gallery and walked towards Ivor's car. But before she reached it, quick footsteps behind her caught up with her and someone roughly grabbed her shoulder.

"Hey," said Vivienne. Turning quickly she saw that it was Maureen.

She took a deep breath. The last thing she wanted was a cat fight outside this upmarket studio. She turned so she was facing Maureen and looked at her questioningly. She was shocked by what she saw. Gone was her veneer of sultriness and sophistication. Her dark eyes were screwed up and she was pulling an angry face. She put her arm out as if to grab Vivienne again, but Vivienne stepped backwards.

"What is it, Maureen?" she breathed.

"Don't act innocent," said Maureen in a loud voice. "That is my man and I'll make sure you *suffer,* until you release him."

Vivienne opened her mouth to say that she wasn't in any way holding Ivor, but closed it again. Maureen was yelling now. "You have made me very angry, lady, and I am not nice when I am angry," she snorted.

Then she turned and disappeared.

Ivor by now had come out of the studio and was making his rapid way over to his car.

"Vivienne, I heard raised voices?" he said.

"It was Maureen. She is not happy that I am with you."

Ivor put his arm around Vivienne, and opened the car door for her. "I had no idea she would follow us when I told the class about mermaid rock and the picture studio," he said. "And to take her anger out on you. ... it's me she should be angry with, but it seems as if she thinks you are in the way of what she wants."

Vivienne was tight-lipped. She had not enjoyed the face to face with Maureen, who seemed to have no idea of decorum, though perhaps it was deliberate, she thought. as Ivor settled her and looked anxiously at her.

"Are you okay, Vivienne?" he asked.

"Not really," said Vivienne. "I'm not used to violent-threatening scenes in public."

Ivor smiled into his beard and patted Vivienne's arm. "I'm sure you stood up beautifully to her, Vivienne," he said, "with such dignity."

At this, Vivienne had to laugh. breaking her sombre mood. "I will need to develop warrior armour, Ivor," she said, "if I have to deal with these threats. Lucky we are leaving tomorrow."

"Yes," said Ivor, "and when we get back and, after lunch, I have to set up the room for the students with a couple of extra places... you and Julie... to paint. It should be lovely for all to use what they have learnt as a creative watercolour." Vivienne was unsettled, knowing Maureen was in the class. Her harsh threatening words were ringing in her ears. Ivor seemed to pick up on her worries.

"Maureen will behave, Vivienne, so please don't worry. You will enjoy the afternoon." He patted her arm and smiled directly at her as he started the car and they drove back to the Convention Centre.

After a quick lunch, Ivor asked Vivienne, "Can you make it up to the Centre on your own or should I come back and fetch you?"

Vivienne smiled. "Ivor, I can manage, thank you. The path is paved and my bag of art materials is not heavy. I'll see you there in a half an hour."

After Ivor had left, Vivienne tidied up, and selected what materials she felt she needed so that her bag was not heavy. She had on flat walking shoes, jeans and a long-sleeved shirt. She added a wrap as she wasn't sure what the weather would be like after the course was over.

Vivienne still had uneasy thoughts about Maureen, who would be part of this afternoon's workshop. Still she decided to take Lady Lavender's advice and to stop her head from thinking thoughts and to stay with her attention simply on the moment. It wasn't easy, but she made herself look at the door as she locked it, and the path as she walked up towards the Convention Centre ... there were small beds of wild flowers on either side that she had not really noticed. It was good to remind herself of the need to be constantly aware.

Soon she had reached the foyer of the Convention Centre and entered. She saw a notice on the door to her left saying, *'Artists Workshop'* and cautiously she opened the door. There was Ivor. He noticed her immediately and came with a smile to greet her.

Vivienne noticed a number of large tables each with two chairs. And most of them were occupied. Students looked up and smiled as Ivor took Vivienne's arm and steered her to a table in the front.

"Julie will join you here," he said, "and you will meet the other students at tea time. We are about to start."

There were a few empty chairs, but the door opened and in came a student followed by Julie, who smiled when she saw Vivienne and Ivor.

"Here's your place, Julie," said Ivor, and Julie sat down next to Vivienne, who felt very relieved. She didn't want to look around for Maureen, but didn't have to, because on the chair at the adjoining table sat Maureen.

Ivor was speaking and all were listening. He was smiling at his class. "I know you have had great success each day with different elements of watercolour painting," he said, "and now it is your chance to paint any scene you like, using any of the skills you have learnt and there are many ... big brush's many manoeuvres, rushing water, trees of all kinds, flat meadow lands, and skies of all kinds. I have put an A4 piece of 300g watercolour paper on each desk and you have water. I'll be playing soft baroque music so there is to be no talking ....

"We will stop in an hour and a half for a tea break and then for another half an hour to finish off. I'd like all to display their pictures at the end and trust you will all be able to use these new skills for many beautiful paintings. And it any of you like to get in touch with me afterwards and tell me how you are getting on with your painting, my business card with contact details and address is on my desk. You are welcome to take one. " He smiled and nodded to the students.

With that, he switched on soft baroque music and nodded to Vivienne. She knew this was to calm her worries that Maureen, sitting just a few feet away, would cause no problems. Vivienne wasn't so sure.

Vivienne would dearly have loved to close her eyes and get creative prior to putting paint on her paper, but she was aware of Maureen, who in a sibilant whisper drowned to all except Vivienne by the music, hissed, "Clever move taking up art so you could trap him, but I'll be moving in soon, just watch me." This disoriented Vivienne, who thought in horror of Maureen turning up at Ivor's place with her luggage. She sat in a mild stupor while Maureen hissed out, "And that's not all . you'll find out what bad things happen to you for moving in on my man."

Ivor who had been walking about between the desks was again in front of the class. He looked sternly at Maureen, who turned her attention to her piece of watercolour paper and made a few meaningless strokes on it.

Vivienne still did not feel creative, but was jolted back into what they were to be doing by Julie, who whispered, "Is everything all right?"

Vivienne whispered back, "Not really. I'll tell you about it at tea."

And, somehow, that short interplay with Julie was enough to bring her back to the present and her piece of watercolour paper.

Not feeling very creative, she nevertheless used her big brush to paint the whole piece with clean water and then began idly dropping in colours. She didn't have any idea of what she was to paint, but the feeling of just letting the paint do its own thing was strong. Probably a sky, she thought, giving more than two-thirds of the paper over to the colours mixing by themselves, forming an interesting late-afternoon sky with some red, orange, deep navy-blue and a nice sky-blue. The yellow she added gave the picture a wonderful halo-like quality to banks of late afternoon clouds in a sky with a setting sun. Or so, Vivienne thought, as she immersed herself in the love of painting. Maureen was forgotten, for the moment, anyway.

Maureen obviously had no intention of being forgotten, because when

Ivor was again at the back of the class, she whispered, "This man and I made a pact to marry. You are in the way, but that's not going to stop me. Watch your back, lady ... "

As Ivor was walking back towards the front of the class, Maureen desisted and turned her attention to the uninspired landscape she was painting.

By tea time Vivienne had a painting of a wonderful late-afternoon sky, and knew that after tea, she had just a simple foreground to complete. She felt happy in her soul. Maureen's taunts were obliterated by the thrill of painting

Soon it was time for a break. "Fifteen minutes," said Ivor, "then back to work."

Vivienne nodded to Julie and each took their cup of coffee and small cakes through to a table at the end of the foyer, hidden in a corner so that Maureen's roaming eyes did not see them.

"Now tell me what all this is about," urged Julie.

"Briefly, Ivor and I are great friends. He invited me on this retreat as cook and bottle-washer, and he was surprised when one student said she knew him from long ago. Maureen Grylke. Ivor can remember nothing of his late teenage years, but she insists he promised to marry her and I'm in the way. Ivor suggested he recognize me as his partner, on a personal level, hoping that would deter her, but it only infuriated her and now she's taking it out on me."

"Maniacal disposition," murmured Julie. "Take care, Vivienne, she can be dangerous."

Vivienne felt alarmed. "That's rather worrying, Julie," she said. "But I'm not surprised. I think she has got a mental condition."

"No, don't let it trouble you too much. Just take extreme care not to annoy her. And I'd like to keep in touch, Vivienne. Here is my business card with cell number. Maybe we could all do a little road trip tomorrow morning, each with their own art in mind."

"Great idea," said Vivienne. "You have lifted my spirits, Julie. This has become an unwelcome burden. But I do know what I need to do."

She didn't elaborate, but suddenly the image of Lady Lavender had arrived in her head. Lady Lavender would know what Vivienne would need to do to free herself from the heavy cloud that now hung over her.

"The road trip is a great, idea, Julie, for some later date. But what about tomorrow? We are leaving, but could delay until the afternoon."

"And I could find someone to look after my studio and we can all go down to Mermaid Rock. to paint, photograph, or simply to relax."

"Yes," said Vivienne, "I know there is a special healing property in that space where land meets the ocean and I think that a morning down there with the three of us would be a wonderful conclusion to this week."

"Time for the break is up," boomed Ivor. "Back to your paintings, Artists, please."

Vivienne and Julie came out from their hidey hole behind the draped curtains to see the angry face of Maureen, as if she'd been looking for Vivienne. Vivienne did the unthinkable. She smiled at her, to Maureen's obviously intense annoyance.

"Think you're clever, don't you?" she hissed as she passed Vivienne to take her place at her table.

Vivienne looked innocently ahead, but had a delicious feeling that this was a one-up for her. I'm not going to be intimidated by her, she said to herself, and settled down as the soft music started to play to complete her foreground, *a simple foreground if you have a busy sky*, she remembered so it was easy to lightly paint in some soft beach sand reflecting some of the afternoon's warm rays with some pieces of driftwood lying on the sand.

Vivienne felt a sense of elation. She had done a lovely watercolour painting under trying circumstances. Most of the students were completing their work and Ivor indicated the long blackboard in the front, which had a small tray running beneath its entire length to hold up the paintings.

"Please put your pictures up against the blackboard," he said, "and then just sit in your seat until all the paintings are up. Then, if you wish, you can all come closer to look at techniques and colours and enjoy each other's works. There are no prizes, just the prize of feeling good about your abilities after a week of learning new methods."

The students started chatting as they walked up to the blackboard and surveyed each other's work. Julie's was different as she used her own techniques, but there was a charm about the dusty road between old trees with a windmill in the distance.

Vivienne stayed close to Ivor, which seemed to deter Maureen, who shot her nasty looks and under her breath whispered, "You haven't heard the last of me."

Vivienne shivered.

"Cold, Vivienne?" asked Ivor with concern.

"No, not really," said Vivienne and was glad to walk out with Julie and Ivor, to see Maureen walk over to her car.

"We have a plan for tomorrow," said Vivienne. "We didn't ask you but I'm sure you will like it...instead of driving off directly, how about us all meeting up at the beach below, I can draw, Julie can photograph. We can all relax, especially you, Ivor, after your week of teaching. How does that sound?"

Ivor looked a bit taken aback, but smiled at Vivienne. "I see you and Julie mean to keep in touch," he said, "but she's a good influence and an artist and a nice person so I am happy with your plans for tomorrow morning."

To Vivienne's horror, Maureen had not yet left and walked up to Vivienne, saying in a sibilant whisper, "Watch your back, lady, and watch your nightly sleep. It isn't going to be that good." And, with a mean smile, she got into her car and drove away.

Vivienne always felt unnerved at these sly verbal attacks and again shivered slightly. *What could Maureen do*? She knew she had to see Lady Lavender.

But that could only happen after tomorrow when they were back in Kalk Bay.

For now, she got into Ivor's car and was glad to have him drive her down to the cottage. She did her best to stay in the moment, but it wasn't easy.

"You look perturbed, Vivienne," said Ivor, as they got out of the car. "I'd say we best go back up to the Convention Centre and have a last enjoyable supper there. It will save you preparing anything now. How does that sound?"

Vivienne smiled. "Perfect, Ivor." So shortly after that, Vivienne, wearing a nice thick jacket against the early evening chill, and Ivor were back at the Centre for a tasty dinner in a relaxing atmosphere.

Back in the cottage, both she and Ivor were busy with packing up things ready to drive off after a simple breakfast.

"We will spend just the morning down at the beach," said Ivor, "and as soon as we leave, we can find a roadside café for lunch."

So the next morning, after the last bit of tidying up and a simple breakfast, they locked up the cottage. Vivienne looked at it regretfully

"It has been a lovely week, thanks, Ivor," she said. "I have so enjoyed it all."

Ivor smiled. "Most of it, yes," he said and gave Vivienne a playful hug. "Julie suggested I drive you to her studio and that we all walk from there. Her path is shorter and less rock-strewn."

With a last regretful look at the Convention Centre with its sprinkling of cottages below it, Vivienne leaned back to enjoy the wind in her short hair. She smiled at Ivor. "What a lovely end to this week," she said.

Ivor turned his car off and drove down the short private road to reach Julie's studio. As he parked his car, Vivienne was astonished to see another car draw up next to them.

Maureen again. Could that woman ever give up her hunt for Ivor?

It was not usual for Ivor to show anger, but now he did.

As Maureen stepped out of her car and locked it, Ivor got out of his car and demanded, "And what is the meaning of this, Maureen? You have no right to follow us."

"I'm not following you," said Maureen, tossing her long dark hair back and glaring at him through her coal-black eyes. "This studio is open to visitors on Sundays."

Vivienne sat in shocked silence. Then as Ivor opened her door, she stepped out. She had on her swimming costume under a loose cotton dress. She picked up her towel and her sketch book and pen. Ivor stood protectively next to her. He turned to lock the car then taking Vivienne's arm and ignoring Maureen, he walked with her to Julie's shop. Maureen followed closely behind.

Inside the studio, Julie took one look at the scene before her eyes and indicated to Ivor and Vivienne to go through a door into an adjoining room.

Once inside, she locked the door and said in shock, "The effrontery of that woman! Following you here. I guess to have one last go at you Vivienne."

"She's not finished with me," said Vivienne. "She indicated I needed to watch my back and my dreams at night. She is terrifying."

"Well, let's not worry about her," said Julie. "My staff will deal with her and we can go through the back yard to Mermaid's Rock below. Let's leave bad things behind us," She smoothed back her long golden hair and smiled at Ivor and Vivienne. "I am so looking forward to spending a couple of hours with you and, look, I have a picnic basket packed and ready ... and I have my own cameras ... and yes, I have my sketch book, and you, Ivor?" She looked at Ivor pertinently.

"I have just myself," said Ivor, with a smile. "I will enjoy the sea and the sand."

Soon, with Ivor carrying the picnic basket, the three made their way down the little twisty path that was a short cut to the beach. Vivienne drew a breath of pure delight as she saw the blue of the ocean with the white waves crashing against black rocks and sending up a spray of foam.

A few seagulls flew overhead, giving off their piercing cries. The sky was a wonderful shade of blue. The day was calm and the sun shone brightly on a sparkling sea. Soon they were on the soft sands of the beach.

Vivienne knew this was going to be the perfect ending to an unpredictable week.

"Right, I'll spread our repast out on this rock," said Julie, getting out biscuits and cheese, glasses and a bottle of champagne. "To a great week and new friendships that are precious," she said. "And let's toast the mermaid of Mermaid Rock."

Ivor opened the champagne and poured champagne into three glasses. They all clinked glasses and smiled warmly at one another. Later, Vivienne wandered amongst the rocks and paddled in the sea, getting wet with the foam of breakers and laughing ... With precious moments spent by each in following their own art form ...

photographs, sketches or simply just absorbing it all on Ivor's part ... And Vivienne was happy.

She had things to do, but those would happen when she got home. For now, being in the moment with two good friends and some light snacks, the sea and the sun, was enough.

"No mermaid," quipped Vivienne. "You were the nearest thing to a mermaid when I saw you the other day."

Despite no mermaid, the time they spent together on the beach was exactly what Vivienne needed. Later that morning, she and Ivor waved goodbye to Julie. Vivienne was relieved to see that Maureen's car had gone, but she still had that niggling worry at the back of her mind that Maureen really could do bad things to her.

The drive home was pleasant, and Vivienne thanked Ivor profusely for a most enjoyable week. He helped carry her bag up the steps to her back door, and saw her safely inside. He waved goodbye to her and Vivienne was left alone.

That night, she had dreadful nightmares, such as she had never had before. Monstrous and evil people were taunting her and an evil green face with long tendrils for fingers wanted to wind around her throat. She woke several times in a fright. As usual, she saw dawn break over the sea and, at the same time, she knew a visit to Lady lavender was the first thing she wanted to do.

After six months of ever-increasing closeness with Ivor, she now had his cell number. Although she infrequently phoned him, this morning she knew she needed him to come with her to Lady Lavender.

He answered his cell, sounding ruffled.

"Good morning, Vivienne, I'm in the middle of a crisis," he said.

"Oh Ivor, that's what I phoned you for, to help me with a personal crisis."

"This is one I'm sure you won't want to hear, Vivienne. Maureen is at my gate with her suitcases and she says she's moving in."

Vivienne nearly dropped the phone, her own woes forgotten.

"Ivor how dreadful. What are your doing about it?"

"That's just it, I'm dealing with it now, Vivienne. Maybe I phone you back or better still I may drive to see you. Because I see a way out. My car is in the garage, which has a side entrance. I can get in the car, raise the doors electronically and simply drive out, leaving Maureen at the side gate." And he gave a relieved laugh. "Just solved my problem, Vivienne," he said, "but it's been quite a wake-up call."

Ivor rang off and Vivienne looked at the phone in horror. Maureen at his gate with her suitcases ,.. just as she said, she intended just moving in with him.

Vivienne shook her head. There must be something seriously wrong with Maureen to believe in her fantasy so strongly. Vivienne felt unsettled, so she walked about her small townhouse just to keep herself from wallowing in bad thoughts …

Chapter 6

It wasn't long before she heard the sound of a car outside, then the opening and shutting of a car door, the ping as it was locked and then footsteps hurrying towards her back door. She was ready with the door open when Ivor reached the top step.

His bearded face broke into a smile as he saw Vivienne, and as he stepped inside, he hugged her.

"I needed to do that," he said, releasing her, "simply because I am so overwrought with having Maureen arrive. It is all so unexpected. Just ever so luckily, I did not open the garden gate, though I did go up to see what was the matter. The matter was two large suitcases she said she was bringing into the house."

"I've waited all these years for you. Ivor, and I'm moving in. That's what she said."

"And you said?" queried Vivienne.

"I said, 'No, Maureen, you are *not* moving in. that is not happening.' She started to raise her voice as she did with you, Vivienne, but I simply turned on my heel and went back to the house and left her there, shouting. Then you phoned and I discovered a way out. And left her with her suitcases at my gate." He gave a deep sigh. "How I wish she would give up her fantasy, which I cannot remember at all."

"That's just it, Ivor, please come with me to Lady Lavender. I'm sure Maureen is doing something hocus pocus to me at night as I had most awful nightmares last night. So we both have problems and both have to do with Maureen."

"First, what about a cup of coffee?" asked Ivor. "You know it's not just the coffee I come for." Ivor looked at Vivienne and they both laughed.

"Of course not," said Vivienne. "Today you and I both have problems both to do with one Maureen and I suggest we both visit Lady Lavender. Do you mind? I had a dreadful night last night."

"And I had a dreadful morning, today," quipped Ivor, now able to smile about it all. "I wonder if Maureen is still at my gate. She has that kind of determination that makes me think she's still there."

Vivienne shook her head. "So she meant what she said. She's moving in with you."

"Certainly not," said Ivor. "We will see what Lady Lavender suggests. Meanwhile you do make good coffee," he said as he took a sip. There was a feeling of accord as they both sat silently drinking the coffee.

"Are we walking there?" asked Ivor.

"I wouldn't know how to get there any other way," said Vivienne, putting the two cups in the sink. "So, are you ready, Ivor?"

Ivor was and cheerily took Vivienne's arm as they crossed the street and walked towards the little lane the other side of the railway line, leading down towards the sea and the fisherman's cottage. Vivienne liked this new closeness with Ivor, which had really only developed during the last week and mostly because of Maureen. So she had caused to happen the very thing Maureen didn't want. "Her man" developing a closeness with another woman.

When the path narrowed, Ivor let go of Vivienne's arm, leading the way down the narrow twisting path. Vivienne remembered to shift her attention to the walk, to the houses on either side, the trees and gardens and then to the glint of water as the waters of False Bay came into view. In a very short time, they had turned into the corner of land where Lady Lavender's cottage was and Vivienne smiled as she saw the big brass door knocker. Nothing she was now afraid of.

Vivienne eyed the lavender bushes and the roses climbing up the trellis as she knocked on the door. It was shortly opened by Lady Lavender, who smiled at Vivienne and Ivor. She was dressed in a long gown of deep royal blue. Her dark hair was arranged neatly in a bun on top of her head. Her gimlet eyes that burned with a hidden light were observing Vivian.

"It's good to see you both," she said. "Please do come in. You know the drill .,, kitchen first to fetch ourselves a cup of tea and cookies, chocolate chip today, and then let's get seated so we can talk."

The kettle was soon boiling, the ginger tea made, and each with a plate of chocolate chip cookies and a cup of ginger tea made the way to Lady Lavender's lounge. Vivienne looked around it. She knew it so well by now, and when the big black cat came out from behind a chair, Vivienne knew that the family was in place and ready for a heart-to-heart chat.

"We've just come back from a week's painting course that Ivor gave," she started.

"Yes , and how did it go?" asked Lady Lavender.

"Very well," said Ivor. "The students all have skills now they didn't have a week ago".

"Excellent," said Lady Lavender. "And Vivienne ... did she take part?"

"Not until the last day," said Vivienne. "I had all day to please myself, paint or walk around, enjoying the energies of the place."

"I'm glad to hear that," said Lady lavender. "But what is troubling you so deeply .... Because it is obvious that something is."

Vivienne had a strong suspicion that Lady Lavender knew but wanted her to put words to it.

"There was this one student on the course who said she had known Ivor when they were teenagers and that he was committed to her in marriage ... and I that I had got in the way."

Lady Lavender's eyebrows shot up. She nodded. "Quite a problem for both of you, I see."

"Yes," chipped in Ivor. "She was adamant that I knew her when we were both seventeen, but I have no memory of it at all."

"I believe you," said Lady Lavender. "When deep trauma hits us, we often block out all memory of it. But I want you, Ivor, to close your eyes and go back in time to when you were seventeen."

Ivor looked startled.

"I mean it," said Lady Lavender. "It is quite possible then you can see if she is telling the truth or not."

"How do I do that?" asked Ivor.

"Simply do not open your eyes, but sit still and just wait. Let us see if anything reveals itself to you. Close your eyes, Ivor, close them and breathe deeply, hold your breath and let it out. And repeat this seven more times."

There was silence in the room. A deep silence, as Ivor sat with his eyes shut. He gave a startled jump. And then said in a deep whisper, "Oh, no, so it did happen."

Vivienne wanted so badly to ask what did happen, but had learnt not to talk out of turn.

Ivor sat, eyes shut, hunched up as he whispered, "You betrayed me." And he gave a deep shudder. Vivienne was worried. But Lady Lavender shook her head, indicating that Vivienne should keep quiet.

Ivor sat for a long time with his eyes shut. "I'm reliving it," he said shaking slightly. "It's horrible. Horrible.

Maureen was right, but also terribly wrong." Then suddenly with a big sigh, Ivor opened his eyes and looked sadly at Lady Lavender and Vivienne.

Neither said anything, waiting for Ivor to talk. He closed his eyes again. There was silence in the room. Lady Lavender and Vivienne waited. "Yes, I have had a flashback to myself at seventeen, tousled blond hair, very much the young artist. And Maureen did live next door. She betrayed me to my father as she said, who wanted me to take up boxing. And he beat me senseless. Nearly murdered me. Maureen created that drama and, yes, I believe she rescued me. I don't remember that she wanted me to marry her when she was eighteen. I don't remember that at all. I still don't remember what happened to me after that until I was apprenticed to Gem Huckleberry, a serious artist. But I have told you that. So the middle part is true. But not I think the promise to marry. That I don't remember."

"Quite right," said Lady Lavender. "A woman that determined to possess you heart and soul can make up anything and believe it, too."

"Believe it all her life and even now," said Ivor. "So bits of my past are appearing."

"You need to do some heavy cleansing work," said Lady Lavender. "I will give you some herbs to put in water and to drink. There is much that needs cleansing to let you go free of this past," said Lady Lavender.

Ivor looked relieved. Then he chuckled. "Lady Lavender this lady is right now at my gate with two large suitcases. She told me she is moving in with me."

Lady Lavender chuckled too. "No need to worry, Ivor. You have partially released yourself from her grip. The herbs will do the rest. She will not be at your gate when you return."

Then she turned to Vivienne.

"And your problems are connected, aren't they?"

"Yes, they are," said Vivienne. "That woman attacked me for stealing her man as she called Ivor." And Vivienne looked at Ivor as she spoke, then burst out. "She said I was to watch my back and that bad things would happen to me. And Lady Lavender, I had the most appalling night last night with dreams of monstrous creatures and evil people that kept me awake. She must somehow have sent bad vibes my way."

"Yes, Vivienne, she has and it will take you a bit of time to clear these away. She has sent psychic tendrils to you and you will have to sever these tendrils. There is a special method whereby you entwine yourself with her and then cut the tendrils."

Vivienne looked horrified. "Is it as bad as that?"

"I'm afraid so," said Lady Lavender. "That woman has really got it in for you, but you can be free of her. I will explain exactly what you are to do, and after perhaps another few bad nights, you can sever the connection. I will explain to you."

Vivienne looked at Ivor, who was still recovering from what had been revealed to him. He had a bemused expression on his face.

Lady Lavender noticed it and said, "Ivor, let it go. You are here now in this room with me and Vivienne. The past is the past. This moment is all that matters." Ivor jerked to an upright position and he smiled slowly.

"Yes, Lady Lavender you are quite right and my present is very beautiful. Being here with you and Vivienne in this charming fisherman's cottage that intrigued me so much that I had to paint it."

"Yes, yes," said Lady Lavender, "you have much to be grateful and happy about. Now let's see how we can help Vivienne."

Vivienne was looking anxious. "Lady Lavender, I've had horrible niggling thoughts where Maureen constantly intrudes on my thoughts."

"Yes, dear, deliberate, as you have foiled her carefully manufactured plan to entrap Ivor." She nodded at Ivor. "Luckily Ivor is out of that trap, but you are still in it. People who deal in the dark side are able to entwine themselves in the affairs of others, but if you listen carefully, you can cut these diabolical tendrils she has sent your way."

Vivienne felt startled. "It sounds bad, Lady Lavender."

"Yes, Vivienne, it is, and you will need to endure a few more days of bad dreams. I suggest go to sleep as late as possible so the torment is reduced."

Vivienne listened in horror.

"But there is a way out of it. You will be dealing with psychic energies. But if you do exactly what I say, you will be alright and the end will be that there will be no more of this woman in your life."

Vivienne was listening intently, leaning forward so as to clearly understand.

"You are to draw a circle around yourself the size of your arm and fingers outstretched. You stand in the centre of that circle drawn on the ground. You do understand, it is drawn on the floor or the ground? Now draw a similar circle that just touches your circle but doesn't cut into it. It is to be the size of this woman with arms and fingers outstretched. In your imagination place her in the centre of that circle. Now colour both these circles with gold that runs right around them both. But keep both you and her in the centre of your circles.

"Please draw another circle inside the gold circles. And this circle is to have a neon blue light starting at the point where the two circles touch and running in a clockwise way first around the circle of the woman demonizing you and then around your circle so that it runs in a figure of eight way. Keep your attention on the blue light running between the two circles. You need to keep this flow of light for at least two minutes. Then you can release the images and get on with daily life. At times during the day, you might like to motivate the blue light to keep it charged.

"This won't stop the bad night's sleep, but you will need to endure that for a number of days. In just a few days, the gold and blue lights will have enough power to enable you to cut the cord that is entwining you both. This is done with a sharp knife just where the two circles touch… in severing the cords the two circles become separate. Yours with your own pure life intact and hers with whatever she has in it, but it will no longer concern you. You will be free to enjoy your life as I am sure you are doing with Ivor's help." Lady Lavender smiled at Ivor, who was listening intently.

Vivienne drew a huge breath. "I see I still have a lot to go through," she said, "but I know I can do it as there is a clear positive outcome, which I welcome."

Both Vivienne and Ivor were shaken and Lady Lavender said, "Time for another cup of tea, I can see; and let's take a glance at the sea outside. Look how the waves are breaking on the rocks … so you can know the dangers the fishermen were in, but their skill made sure they were safe."

Vivienne's mind now flew to the sea, the bashing waves and the rocks. She concentrated all her energy on watching the waves as they broke, and then she turned and smiled at Lady Lavender.

"You did that on purpose, didn't you," she said. "To get me back to the moment."

Lady Lavender gave a rare smile. "Quite right, Vivienne, you are a quick learner. What you have just heard and done does not belong to this moment. This moment belongs to us in this room, to Captain, who knows exactly what is happening, don't you, Captain?"

And if cats could talk, Vivienne felt sure Captain was agreeing. She smiled. It felt so comforting to be with Lady Lavender and Captain and Ivor. She was breathing deeply, still mildly upset.

"Time for that tea," said Lady Lavender. "Are you both still happy with ginger tea or would you like a change? Chamomile, perhaps?"

"No, I'm happy with ginger tea," said Vivienne. Ivor nodded in agreement.

"And for eats, I have some excellent whole-wheat muffins, I'm sure you will enjoy."

The tension was broken as they all trooped into the kitchen. Vivienne looked up at the black beams showing the underneath of the thatched roof. All reminiscent of a time long ago. But, also, a reminder that she had found a valuable friend in Lady Lavender, who was able to help both her and Ivor with their problems.

But Ivor," Lady Lavender was saying, "you have a lot more of your past to unearth. Perhaps you have enough for now, but maybe another visit in a week would be good … after Vivienne has cut that evil woman out of her life."

The ginger tea and whole-wheat muffins were perfect to break the tensions of what both Ivor and Vivienne had just experienced. But as soon as they were finished, Ivor indicated they were leaving. He had recovered his placid nature and thanked Lady Lavender for her time. Lady Lavender also gave him two small brown paper bags with herbs inside. "You are to add boiling water and to drink them, one in the morning and one at night, to help cleanse your energies."

Ivor took them and thanked Lady Lavender again.

"My pleasure," she said. "I've been watching you both and have been expecting you. And yes, please, if you'd both visit again in a week's time I think we will discover some more hidden things."

She nodded to them both as Ivor and Vivienne took their leave.

Chapter 7

Both Ivor and Vivienne were silent on their walk back to Vivienne's townhouse.

"Would you like to come in for a while," Vivienne asked. as they reached her back door.

"Yes," said Ivor, "I think I'd like that ..." He hesitated then said with a small smile, "Who knows? Maureen may still be standing at my gate."

At this, they both laughed. Strangely, Maureen was drawing them close together. And there was a definite warmth and friendliness in Vivienne's kitchen as Ivor settled on a chair.

"Maybe a cup of hot chocolate?" suggested Vivienne.

"Yes," said Ivor, "with marshmallows. I've never had that before and it's quite delicious."

Soon, they were both sipping hot chocolate with white foaming marsh mallows. "Totally decadent," said Ivor, "but so special."

There was silence as it seemed that neither Vivienne nor Ivor knew what to say next.

"The painting week was good," said Ivor.

"Yes," said Vivienne. "I feel like a new person ... mostly," she added wryly.

"You are going to have to do exactly what Lady Lavender told you to do," said Ivor.

"I know," said Vivienne, "and I'm not looking forward to what I know is going to be a night of bad dreams."

"Don't dwell on what is to happen," said Ivor.

"So right," said Vivienne. "Perhaps I'll paint."

"Yes, painting will absorb you totally," said Ivor. "If you do that, I won't worry too much about you as I know you will be alright. A good afternoon of painting, some warm and filling food to eat, maybe a glass of wine, and keep your mind off what might happen. Though," he said, "I was thinking that what would be nice would be a day out painting somewhere we haven't been to before."

Vivienne cheered up. "I could spend happy hours dreaming of that," she said, "though that I guess is not staying in the moment."

"Where would you like to go, Vivienne, to draw and paint?"

"I think there's an old windmill in Mowbray, I think it is. I'd like to draw that, then paint in a background with a sky."

"That should be easy, but let's do this a bit later on, " said Ivor. "And for me, I'd like it if I could take you somewhere closer where you would like to go." And with a small slightly embarrassed smile he said, "To apologise for making life difficult for you. I never imagined that turning us into a couple would upset Maureen the way it did."

Vivienne looked at Ivor. "To be honest, I like being part of you, Ivor, even if it was just a kind of smoke screen."

Ivor looked at her seriously. "That sounds as if I have been making use of you, Vivienne. I would never do that, I respect you too much and," he hesitated as he said it, "I am also intensely fond of you so to act as if we were a couple was perhaps just my way of pretending it isn't real when I truly love the idea." Then as if he had said too much he stood up. "Vivienne, I'll be off, but be sure to call me should you need me at all. I have recovered from my session with Lady Lavender and though it was a shock, I must say that, in a way, it is a relief ... though I guess there is more to come. And I know you'll get through your problems. Vivienne, be sure to call me should you need me at all."

He stooped and gave Vivienne a sincere and deep hug. Vivienne looked at him with a light in her eyes. That hug felt so warm and was just what she needed. The present was very good. She waved at Ivor as he left. Then kept her mind fixed exactly on what she was doing. Clearing up after the hot chocolate.

She had much to dwell on. Those circles she was to draw. Where was it best? Perhaps in the lounge where there was space on the carpet for two circles. When should she draw them? Perhaps soon, so that she would have started her journey. Then she could give them a push as Lady Lavender had said, so the light around them grew strong. And the sooner the better she thought. I can't wait for the moment when I sever them. She started immediately, moving a small table to make room for two large circles. She drew her circle with her arms outstretched, on the carpet, with a short stick she used sometimes when out walking. Then she drew a similar slightly larger circle that just touched her circle. She poured gold light into both of them then put herself in the centre of her circle. And with a sense of repugnance, she imagined Maureen and put her in the centre of the second circle.

Now to rapidly energise both with blue neon light that started where the two circles just touched, and ran in a clockwise direction first around Maureen... having Maureen in her lounge wasn't easy ... then back and around herself. She saw the blue neon light and made sure it was brilliant and ran easily around the two circles. 'Do it for two minutes,' Lady Lavender had said. 'And then, during the day, give it a kind of kick start to make sure that it builds up strength to stand on its own ... to free you.'

Afterwards, Vivienne went straight to the bathroom and washed her hands thoroughly. She didn't know why, but it felt better. Then with a huge sigh of relief she went to get her painting materials, and then to sit in the dining room at the table and immerse herself in painting. It wasn't easy as her mind wanted to linger on her troubles but, once she had a sheet of watercolour paper laid out, along with her palette and big brush and a nice big puddle of paint, she forgot about everything, except the delight of seeing colours on the paper mix with other colours. What a joy it was to play with paint.

Vivienne was absolved in creating a wonderful deep valley of mist by using very light alizarin crimson so that the light was just tinged with pink. She had mighty mountains towering above the valley and a soft and playful foreground with patches of brightly coloured flowers against a soft green grass background. Working with paints filled her mind so there wasn't room for any bad thoughts. *What a blessing her watercolour painting was!*

She was so absolved in painting that she didn't realise it was past supper time. She decided on something filling tonight. Mashed potatoes with sausage and gravy with vegetables seemed like a good meal to fill her, so she didn't feel hungry later as she had decided to stay up as late as she could. She was feeling a bit unsettled and when the phone rang she jumped. On answering it, she suddenly realised she had not given a thought to Steven for days. Really, how could she be so uncaring?

"Hullo, Steven," she said … her voice didn't have the usual lift to it and Steven noticed.

"What's up Mom?" he asked. "You sounded on a high when I last spoke to you, more than a week ago, but you sound bothered now."

Vivienne wasn't going to start on the whole long story so she fobbed it off to tiredness. "I've just got back from a painting week, Steven," she said.

"I like it when you sound on a high," Steven said. "But now I'm down and you're down which isn't good."

"Steven, why should you be down?" asked Vivienne, holding her breath. *Not more bad news!* She was not ready for whatever it was, but Steven burst out, "It's Mariette."

"Mariette?" said Vivienne, "but you said she was everything you wanted!"

"Yes, Mom, she is but we have serious differences."

"Which are?"

"Yes, but she is pregnant and she has not told her parents yet, because," Steven lowered his voice, "she wants an abortion." He sounded so upset that Vivienne thought he was close to tears.

"Steven … what can I say?" She felt hopeless.

"Nothing Mom, nothing."

Vivienne so wanted to be able to put her arms around Steven … he needed support now and what could she do?... Nothing.

Vivienne stood with the phone in one hand, doing nothing. She could hear Steven's heavy breathing on the other side.

"Have you tried talking to her?" she asked.

"She's too emotional to talk," said Steven. "Just bursts into tears. I don't know what to do."

Vivienne remembered Lady Lavender's advice about minding one's own business so she didn't make any suggestions. Just stood holding the phone. She stood like that for a long time, whilst Steven struggled on the other end to control his emotions then, finally, he said, in a calmer voice, "Thanks, Mom, just by being there, listening I do feel a bit better. I'll say goodbye, but will keep you in the picture."

Vivienne drew a deep breath.

"Steven, thank you for confiding in me," she said. "It makes me feel part of you still."

"Of course. You are my Mom and I will always keep in touch. Bye for now," and he rang off.

Vivienne felt shaken by the news, but she shook her head. *She had enough of her own troubles at the moment.*

Vivienne remembered to keep the blue lights moving in the circles. She wanted the circles strong as quick as possible. For the rest of the evening Vivienne occupied herself by watching two humorous videos that she had seen before.

She still didn't feel tired. But as it was eleven o'clock, she decided to go to bed, anyway, and she decided to keep the light on. Perhaps she would read for a while; reading in bed always made her drowsy.

She showered, got into her pyjamas and climbed into bed. She had an old book with her that usually made her laugh, but tonight it did not seem funny at all. Nevertheless, she kept reading until at last the book slipped out of her hands and deep sleep followed.

At first, she slept without dreaming, but then the nightmares started, A long skinny arm was reaching out to grab her. She pushed at the arm, but it was long and twisty and grabbed her from behind. A voice said gratingly, "I told you to watch your back."

Vivienne woke in fright. She was too wide awake and frightened to go back to sleep, so got up and pottered around the bedroom. Still unable to sleep, she made for the kitchen. Not coffee, that would keep her awake, but perhaps a soothing cup of hot chocolate. With hot chocolate in hand and still wide awake she made for the lounge and for the circles on the floor. It felt stupid but Vivienne was prepared to do anything so she stood in her circle and imagined the blue neon light pulsing with great energy into the two circles. She stood like that for quite some while.

Then the soothing hot chocolate and the soothing blue neon energies made her sleepy and she returned to her bed. Again, she fell easily to sleep and lay in deep sleep until she heard a cackling voice. "I told you to lay off my man." She was awakened by blinding images of ghosts and ghouls. *How horrible.* Again, Vivienne stumbled out of bed. No, I'm not lying here to have all these bad thoughts in my head, she thought. *What to do…?*

Why not paint… in the early hours of the morning for by now it was almost three am?

But Vivienne was so wide awake and so alarmed at the idea of going to sleep again that she put on the neon light she used to work with when painting, and got out her big brush, some paper and some paints. Maybe I just paint those horrible entities and burn them, she thought. I have heard one can do that with unwanted entities.

It was rather a relief to just let the brush pick up any colour it liked and put it on the paper. Black, indigo and fearsome red. And a spiky orange. The colours all mixed together on the paper and Vivienne looked at it with interest. A face was showing, and the face was that of Maureen... she couldn't believe it and thought of the waste of watercolour paper, as she went to the kitchen and stood over the sink and set light to her painting. She watched in horror as the nasty face of Maureen with the piercing black eyes jeered at her from the paper just to be swirled away by hungry flames. Vivienne felt exhausted after this ... and still wide awake. It was really too early for coffee but right now that's what she wanted. A cup of her strong aromatic coffee, which she drank sitting out in the dining-room area next to the stained-glass door with its uplifting picture of a rising sun. Maybe I'll just sit here until dawn breaks, Vivienne thought, and watch the dawn. Then go back to sleep. Maybe Maureen won't be bugging me anymore as her effigy burned so nicely.

So that was her plan of action and surprisingly it worked very well. Though one doesn't normally fall asleep after coffee, Vivienne was so tired that she easily did and slept dreamlessly until the sun was up and her cell phone rang.

Sleepily, she answered it wondering if it was Steven, but no, it was a concerned Ivor asking how her night went.

126

"Why don't you come over for coffee?" she asked, "I am still in my night attire and need to shower and get dressed then I can tell you."

"You sound cheerful," said Ivor, "so that's a good sign, and yes, I'll be over in less than an hour."

Vivienne switched off her cell with a sense of freedom. And she smiled. Ivor for coffee and a good tale to tell him.

In the kitchen, she looked at the ashes which were all that remained of her last painting. She had a hurried breakfast, showered and got dressed and put on the coffee in preparation for Ivor's visit.

When he arrived, he gave her an enormous hug.

"I feel responsible for much of what is happening to you," he said, looking into her eyes. "So, of course I need to know what happened and why you look so cheerful in the face of bad dreams."

"Ah," said Vivienne, "it was quite a night. One I shan't forget in a hurry. I started by staying up late, but eventually fell asleep. Then these long creepy hands came at me, grabbing me. They were bendy and went for my back and there was a voice that whispered hoarsely, "I told you to watch your back" and as it grabbed fiercely at my back, I awoke … I stayed awake a long time and then much later tried to sleep again. This time I slept nicely for a short period of time then the ghoulish voice got into my thoughts, "You are not taking my man" and it came at me with hideous face and colours and I awoke and stayed awake. Then I painted ... and Maureen's face turned up on my painting so I went to the kitchen and I set it alight. Burnt it. Burnt Maureen." And Vivienne jumped up and hugged Ivor. "And I felt free of her. I don't know if I really have stopped things before I cut those cords, but I am sure I will have a better night tonight."

Ivor stood, holding Vivienne in his arms. They felt so close, and Vivienne felt a deep joy. She gave a small laugh. "It didn't feel funny at the time, but it was lovely to see those evil eyes surrounded by real flames that devoured her. Every bit of her." And they looked at one another and both smiled. Ivor's face was full of light and Vivienne felt a joy she hadn't felt in a long time.

Ivor didn't stay long. As he left, he said, "Get as much rest as you can during the day, Vivienne. Then be prepared to be a night owl." He smiled at her, his eyes connecting with hers. "But I know you'll have a better night tonight," he added as he left.

Vivienne thought it would be a good idea to get some fresh air and sun ... and so, after she'd tidied her home, she made for the sea across the way.

At first, she just walked, enjoying the sun on her face; it felt healing and healthy and the slight breeze that ruffled her short hair brought a smile to her face. How I love the wind now, she thought. It blows away all sorts of bad thoughts, letting the healing waters and sunshine fill her soul.

She walked, being aware of her footsteps on soft grass and then on bits of paving. Soon she was by the harbour with the fishing vessels and the yachts with their sails blowing in the wind. It was all so colourful... the brilliant blue sea and sky, the white of the waves and the seagulls and the beautifully painted boats. Vivienne wandered about, just looking and smelling the salty air, feeling the healing of the elements ... she needed to be as strong and as rested as possible. And she meant to have a sleep in the afternoon.

It was an hour or two later when she returned to her home. Her eyes lit up as she saw the sign 'Welcome' outside her back door. She felt a newness in her and carefully climbed the steps and opened the back door. Yes, she would eat and rest, and then prepare her supper, watch some more videos, and stay up as late as she could ... she pulled her mind back to the moment when she saw herself wondering if tonight would be any better than last night. But in her heart, she knew it would be.

On this particular night, Vivienne slept for several hours before an irritated effigy of Maureen came into her head. "Nice try," it spluttered, "but I'm still here." The effigy faded as it said that, but Vivienne awoke, startled, and very aware of what the effigy had said. Again, she felt that trying to go back to sleep was not a good idea. So, she got up and again went to the kitchen and made herself a cup of hot chocolate. "Let me have a midnight feast," she thought. Silly thought but it will give me something to do…. What is there that's nice to eat?

She thought back to being a teenager and the midnight feasts they had, and giggled at the thought. Sardines, condensed milk, what a mixture. No, she would go for some chocolate biscuits, and some ice cream with some apple tart she knew she had. A good feast in the middle of the night was sure to give her indigestion, but the thought of the indigestion was not enough to deter from giving herself this treat. She spent quite a long time, setting it all out. The ice cream in a bowl with lemon curd and cream on top, and the apple tart warmed slightly with cinnamon and thick cream.

She included chocolate biscuits and yet another cup of hot chocolate. She took her midnight feast into the dining room near the stained-glass window… Wrapped in a warm dressing gown she relaxed back in an easy chair and slowly enjoyed her midnight feast. However, the delicious warm apple tart and cream lulled her to sleep as she sat in the easy chair. That lovely sleep was interrupted by a voice in her head that loudly proclaimed, "Ha, so you thought you could escape. I told you, you had a bad time ahead and I may strangle you – just leave my man alone." There was a kind of a shriek, at this point, which jolted Vivienne awake. Very much awake

Vivienne jumped up and walked about, rubbing her eyes. It wasn't as bad as last night, but it still was very disturbing. She didn't paint this night, but sat staring out at the dark sky and very carefully watching her thoughts so that all she was aware of was the dark sky outside, slowly tinging with the pale light of dawn, and nothing else. She was getting good, she noticed, at being able to keep her thoughts on the moment. On nothing ... so that she had peace in her head. In a strange way, she almost heard the demons, whose ghostly voices she heard in her mind, shaking their heads as their strategies just weren't working.

By the time the sun had risen, Vivienne was really tired and went to bed and slept soundly. The daylight helped. She was awoken with the loud ringing of her cell phone. *Steven?* she wondered as she sleepily groped for it.

"Hello," she said.

"Hello, Vivienne," said the deep soft voice of Ivor. "How was your sleep last night? I have been really concerned about you."

Vivienne with her eyes still closed, said, "Better by fifty percent, but the voices still got to me so I only went to sleep after the sun was up."

"And I've disturbed your sleep. I'm so sorry, Vivienne."

"It's nice to talk to you," said Vivienne, her eyes still half-closed.

Ivor continued, "What would you say if I was to come over and spend the night with you? I'm not sure where I could sleep, but I'd like to be near to you. Could we both sleep in the lounge, perhaps?"

Vivienne was digesting the idea. And she sat up in bed and smiled.

"Lovely idea, Ivor, it would be company."

"We could watch videos, or just talk," said Ivor.

Vivienne felt a leap of joy. For Ivor to suggest talking ... "Yes, Ivor, that's very possible. The sofa is big enough for you to lie on it and I could get comfortable in one of those big arm chairs. I'm not sleeping properly, anyway, and the idea of you being there would be a great comfort. Thank you so much for the suggestion. I think it's a wonderful idea."

"Then I'll be over as soon it gets dark," said Ivor. "Don't worry about supper. I'll eat at home."

Vivienne was smiling when Ivor rang off. The bad night was forgotten as she had a hot shower and prepared for the day. She had spare duvets in the cupboard that were cosy, as they were made of feathers. She found two. And two big feather pillows. And arranged them in the lounge. Whilst she was there, she made a two-minute mental tour of blue neon light on the imaginary circles on the floor. How she wished the next few days were over! It was encouraging that last night's disturbances were much less than the previous night. *How lovely to have Ivor with her tonight!*

The day went quickly and soon it was night. Vivienne dressed herself in a warm track suit rather than pyjamas. When Ivor arrived, she smiled as he had had a similar thought and had a dark-green tracksuit on. She smiled as she let him in and they hugged. It was getting the usual thing to do, somehow a consolation in a very testing week.

"See how comfy I've made the lounge," Vivienne said. "But we can watch some movies first if you wish."

"I'm not a great fan of movies," said Ivor. "Let's just see how we get on tucked into our makeshift beds. Perhaps you have some snacks for us?"

"Oh yes," said Vivienne. "I thought of that. Things to nibble... some nuts, biscuits, and cheeses. A sort of cheese and biscuits starters and I've made a flask of hot chocolate," said Vivienne.

It was uplifting and friendly as they sat quite close to one another, nibbling biscuits and chatting.

Ivor said, "I have had excellent feedback from the organisers of the painting week."

"That's great," said Vivienne. "And so, you should. They all did lovely creative paintings on our last afternoon there."

"And they'd like me to do another concentrated course with the outcome of an A3 size painting by all. Of a quality that can be exhibited."

"That's a little off-putting, don't you think?" said Vivienne. "Expecting it to be good enough to be exhibited."

"Not at all," said Ivor. "I know they will all be of that quality."

"Would they be the same students from your last course?" asked Vivienne, her mind jumping to Maureen.

Ivor smiled at her. "I know what you are thinking, Vivienne, and it would not be all of them. I can pick two of the best. Both men. That leaves all the women out. The two men will excel."

"When is this to take place, Ivor?"

"Not immediately. In a few weeks or a month. It will be an advertisement for something much bigger. Having beginners produce quality creative watercolour paintings will be a draw-card for many others, who would love to paint, but are too afraid to. Meantime, I will keep in touch with them and suggest a refresher day-course in a weeks' time." He smiled at Vivienne.

They got on to easy chat about painting and when he was to take Vivienne to sketch and paint the old windmill in Mowbray. Then he asked a surprising question.

"Vivienne, I don't know anything about your life before Kalk Bay," he said. "What did you do and where did you live?"

Vivienne smiled at him.

"This will take all night," she said, "so we won't need movies to occupy us. Let me go back to more than half my life .... I studied to become a teacher, and found a post at which I stayed for twenty years.... It was an elegant girls' finishing school where the principal wanted the students to not only learn academics, but to learn the skills of gracious living. So that if invited out to dinner they would know which spoon to eat with or which fork … when a dinner party takes place, which is rare, but does happen.

"Also, to know how to sit correctly, stand correctly, walk with ease, but be elegant, how to chat easily with strangers. And a lot of things that normal schools don't teach young people."

"That sounds intriguing," said Ivor, smiling into his beard.

"You're laughing, Ivor," she said admonishing him lightly. "You I guess were a Bohemian."

"I don't know what I was," said Ivor, "but artists are by nature unconventional. They are there to paint the essence of a flower, a building, a ship, a person, and outer trappings are a mere inconvenience."

He and Vivienne got into an energetic conversation about what was real. What really mattered in life.

"Harmlessness, I'd say, kindness, compassion, caring, and deep observation of a person or situation, I'd say are the essentials of life. Not the elegant dinner parties Vivienne."

"Maybe not," Vivienne defended her school, "but if one gets thrown unexpectedly into some situation that one has had some preparation for, isn't it better than feeling lost and behaving incorrectly?"

"That's what I'm talking about," said Ivor. "What do you call behaving incorrectly."

"Well, I guess by standards laid down just by the way people do things …"

"That's what I mean… people are not being who they truly are, when you do things because that's the way it's done," said Ivor.

"How did you learn to fit in?" asked Vivienne.

"Now that's a long story," said Ivor. "I can't tell you much of it, because I don't remember much of it. This is what Maureen was going on about … but I do remember that school made no sense to me. It was boring and I just wasn't interested. But I found art… paint … artists and what they had done in the past and they inspired me. Particularly I wanted to create my own genre, which as an adolescent young boy is rather too ambitious. And that's when I started acting oddly, as Maureen said. Wanting to paint red clouds and leaving one's art class and looking for another art class, until my father found out what I was doing." He hesitated then carried on. "I know a little part of it from what happened at Lady Lavender's house, but I've remembered a bit more.. I remember that Maureen did take me to her friends, who were supposed to look after me, but they had no idea how to handle me…none at all…and I ran away.

"I just ran away without knowing where I was going. I bumped into an artist sitting at an intersection, painting the scene around him with deft sure strokes and with colours not of the scene, but of his imagination, so that what he produced didn't look at all like what he was looking at. I was shabbily dressed, with long hair, but something about my passion for this man's way of painting intrigued him and he chatted with me, found I was running away with no idea of where I was going. And he took me home, gave me shelter and an apprenticeship in art." Ivor smiled at Vivienne. "But I didn't learn all those niceties you are talking about. I learnt about colour, light, colour harmonies, and much else of great importance to the artist."

Vivienne listened, intrigued.

Ivor continued, "But I didn't learn how to do small talk with people. It was all about art and techniques, so I am not good socially." He gave Vivienne an extra-special smile.

Instead of feeling sleepy, Vivienne was wide awake, even though it was getting on for midnight.

The evening without sleep, but with Ivor for company was surprising. She wanted to know more about Ivor, but at this point he yawned and rubbed his eyes.

"Vivienne, I'm going to doze now. If you do the same and have bad dreams, wake me. And thanks for the chat."

Ivor closed his eyes and Vivienne watched as he almost immediately fell asleep ... his breathing changed and she looked at this big man, sleeping soundly on her lounge sofa. Would she be able to get to sleep that quickly? And did it matter if she didn't? She actually thought it was a good idea to simply stay awake, which she did for the next fifteen minutes, turning over in her mind, facts Ivor had just given her. Then sleep took over and she went into slumber land. She lay cuddled in her armchair with the feather duvet tucked around her.

For quite a long time, her mind was peaceful then suddenly an image of a leering Maureen popped into her mind. And with malice in her black eyes it screeched in her head, "You think you've got him, but you haven't."

The long skinny green arms and hands with claws outstretched, came straight at her face. Vivienne woke up, gasping.

"Horrible, horrible," she groaned, at which Ivor immediately awoke.

"Vivienne, what is it?" he asked.

"A nightmare," she whispered.

"Horrid! Maureen with long skinny green arms and fingers with long claws on them and taunting black eyes ... screeching inside my head." She was so upset that Ivor pulled his duvet off himself and went over to Vivienne. He put his arms around her and she put her head on his shoulder.

"It is too awful," she said. "It didn't last as long this time, but so horrible, I am not going back to sleep again tonight." Vivienne was resolute on that. She sat up straight and Ivor moved away from her. Then she added, "No, Ivor, you sleep. You need it. I don't. I have learnt how to quiet my mind. I will take my duvet into the dining room and sit by the glass door and wait for sunrise. Please don't worry about me. I want to do it this way."

"Thanks, Vivienne," said Ivor, "I actually do need my sleep so if that is okay with you, I'll tuck up on the sofa again."

He was soon sound asleep as Vivienne took her duvet and herself to the dining room and sat in a chair opposite the glass door. She tucked the duvet around her so that she felt cosy and could even have gone back to sleep, except that she willed herself not to. Instead, she sat practicing awareness and peace, and nothingness in her head. The glass-stained door of the rising sun was inspiring and by concentrating on that and watching what she was thinking, she was able to get a peaceful head even if she was very short of sleep. She sat like that for an hour or more, watching the glory of the dawn.

It was only when the sun broke through that she went back to the lounge where Ivor was still fast asleep. She smiled as she looked at him, deciding to leave him as he was. She made her way to her bedroom. Now that the sun was up and the night elements had given over to daytime, she knew she could sleep without worry. Still in her tracksuit she climbed into bed and was soon fast asleep. It was about ten o'clock when she awoke.

The first thing she did was to put on the coffee and then she went to check on Ivor and was surprised to see him just waking up. She wanted badly to tousle his hair, but thought better of it and instead said politely, "I hope you were comfortable, Ivor."

He stretched, scratched his beard and smiled. "Perfectly so, thanks Vivienne. I slept much better than I do at home." Then he added, "Is that coffee I smell?"

"Yes, it is," said Vivienne. "It will be ready in a few minutes."

Whilst he and Vivienne were sitting in the kitchen enjoying their coffee, he said, "I'll be off now... half the day has gone. but I will come again tonight after dark... will that suit you, Vivienne?"

"Very much so," said Vivienne, "and thank you. Your presence helped hugely." They smiled at one another.

Chapter 8

Steven phoned. Vivienne was now not entirely enthusiastic about Steven's phone calls. He had troubles and she was letting him sort them out for himself.

She answered the phone in a calm way. "Hi, Mom, Steven here. How are you today?"

Then without waiting for her to reply, he said, "I know you so well, Mom, and I'd say things are okay with you."

Vivienne felt like saying, *If only you knew*. But she didn't. At that moment, they were okay and she agreed with Steven. "Yes, I'm good thanks, Steven, and how it is going with you?" She held her breath. The last time he was not okay.

Steven swallowed. Vivienne heard that and waited.

"Still upside down, Mom, but at least Mariette is not crying so much."

"And the abortion?" Vivienne hardly liked to ask this.

"She still wants one," said Steven, "but we are both being less emotional now. I am trying to see things from her point of view. Though she isn't seeing them from mine. I understand that it will get in the way of her career... having a baby to give birth to, then to nurture and care for it. This is without even telling her parents, who could have a lot to say about it. It's a very tricky situation, Mom."

"Well," said Vivienne, "at least you are more stable emotionally than the last time I spoke to you."

She was relieved that Steven didn't want to stay on the phone for long and rang off shortly.

The day was uneventful and Vivienne was more on the side of the angels as she briefly, ever so briefly, thought with joy of the time she had with Ivor, the previous evening. Her horrid nightmare was nothing in comparison to having her tutor and friend open up and talk to her as a person. She hoped more of the same would happen that evening.

Soon it was dark and Ivor arrived, shaking his overcoat as he took it off. He had on a different tracksuit, this time, a snowy white one, which was unusual for a man. She was wearing a navy tracksuit. She greeted Ivor then looked at his tracksuit.

"White, that's unusual, Ivor. Where did you get it? And why white?"

"Well, tracksuits can be any colour," said Ivor. "I saw this white one and I liked it. It's as simple as that."

"Well, it's really nice. Looks cosy. too," she said, as she led Ivor through to the lounge.

"To tell you the truth, I just felt like being different."

Vivienne nodded. "You've made your point, Ivor," she said with a smile. "It is different."

"And white is a good colour when you're dealing with evil," he said seriously.

Vivienne looked at him in surprise and said, "You do take these things seriously then?"

"Oh yes," said Ivor. "I have no doubt that Maureen means you harm. So, I am bringing light and comfort, I hope, Vivienne."

"Thank you, Ivor. It was such a treat having you here last night. The sofa is waiting for you again."

Ivor settled himself, at first just sitting on the sofa with the duvet over his legs. Vivienne settled in a big arm chair and pulled her duvet over her legs.

"Well, we are both comfortable now," said Ivor, "and I see you have an array of goodies. I love candied fruit. Is that watermelon? I do enjoy it," and he helped himself to a big piece of pale green crystallized melon. In between his enjoyment of it, he said, "Vivienne, let us continue with our stories of ourselves. I enjoyed your story of your teaching and grooming young ladies to fit into society." He smiled into his beard.

Vivienne saw this and said in slight indignation, "It was a worthy cause, Ivor."

"Oh yes, I know," he said. And Vivienne wasn't sure if he meant it or was being humorous. "But before the school, you must have had a number of years of life."

"Oh yes," said Vivienne. "I took up teaching directly after leaving school. It was during my last year at

143

teachers' college that I met Paul and we were married when I was twenty. Steven was born shortly afterwards. My early years of teaching were in government schools, children of all ages." Vivienne shook her head.

"Didn't you like it?" asked Ivor.

"Oh yes, I loved the teaching, but, sometimes, the children got a bit much for me. Those early teens when kids think they know it all … Paul was a teacher, too, and he took me out of the rougher government school to a nice area in the country where he had a post at a boys' high school, a boarding school, and he got us a house on the property. It was lovely. We were there for many years. Steven grew up there and attended a small village school. I did some part-time teaching, but was mostly at home."

She paused.

"You are sad," said Ivor.

"No, not really," said Vivienne. "Just remembering that my husband, Paul, had a massive heart attack and passed away suddenly. That was when I had to take charge of my own life and of Steven's as well. He was about fifteen then and had to become the man of the house …. Yes, we had to leave Merrievale and I bought my own home in Cowies Hill. Paul had a large life insurance that meant I had no financial worries. I lived in Cowie's Hill for many years. The teaching job I got there was when I went to this girls' finishing school. And I only left the house early this year when I sold up to come to Kalk Bay."

"What interests did you have in Cowies Hill?" Ivor asked.

"Not many," said Vivienne. "I am a private person so didn't mix socially ... I enjoyed my garden and the hadidahs ... and many different birds on my property. And I had three very different friends, who each visited once a week." She smiled as she recalled them. "And what they all had to say about me coming to Kalk Bay means I can never really phone them."

"Why is that?" asked Ivor.

"Because I know they wouldn't want to hear all the good things about being here." She smiled at Ivor. "And you are one of them, Ivor," she said, without really meaning to.

"Oh, thank you," said Ivor, looking almost proud.

"So now you have put the dots together," said Vivienne.

"And the Steven part?" asked Ivor.

"Oh, Steven," said Vivienne. "He promised to do all sorts of little things for me, which is why I came here." She laughed. "It was that silly child-lock that has caused me problems twice. And that is why I am here, and it is also why Steven is not here, because he met this girl, Mariette, who came over from France as a delegate of his company, supposedly just for a week to check us out. But Steven landed up going back to France with her... he was so enamoured of her that he told me, once he was there, that he was in love and would probably relocate to France."

Vivienne looked pensive and Ivor said, "So you have had a lot of changes in your life just recently, Vivienne."

"Yes, I have," she said. "And I must say that I didn't think I was going to like Kalk Bay, but I do now, most definitely. It is an artists' haven, then there is the bay and the sunrise and the people... and you." She smiled at Ivor. "Now, Ivor, it's your turn. I want to hear a bit more of your story."

Ivor shook his head. "No nothing more, but I do remember I was a passionate youngster with fairly long blond hair ... and I didn't fit in anywhere. Nothing made sense to me and, yes, I remember Maureen did get me drinking. So that, too, infuriated my father. but she told him about my art, so she almost deliberately caused my troubles. And yes, I guess she was keen on me. I was not the size I am now..." he chuckled... "but I was tall and I guess nice-looking with that blond longish arty hair. And I listened to Maureen. I didn't have friends and, as I remember, just a father, I don't know what happened to my mother, but my father wasn't understanding at all. Maureen let me down. I certainly don't remember saying anything about marrying her. I was far too young for that. But all that is a great muddle and lost inside me, because I guess it was all so traumatic."

Time had gone by quickly. The crystallised fruit was all gone. The chocolates and biscuits, as well, and, that night, Vivienne had poured each a glass of sherry. "To keep us warm and let me get to sleep easily," she said, "and hopefully to have no bad dreams."

She looked at Ivor and said seriously, "I am still energizing those two circles with blue light. I am sure I can cut the cord on Day 6. I am on Day 5 now, so there's only one more day ...Then we will go to see Lady Lavender," said Vivienne firmly. "For both you and for me."

Ivor had spread himself out over the sofa. He had to bend his legs slightly, but this big snowman in the white tracksuit made Vivienne chuckle.

"What's so funny?" asked Ivor, as he pulled the duvet up to his chin.

"Just seeing a snowman on my couch," said Vivienne.

Both laughed and Ivor said, "Well, goodnight, Vivienne, this snowman is now getting some sleep, and I hope you do, too."

"Thanks," said Vivienne, "I'm not quite ready to sleep. I'll do some more circles on the carpet if it doesn't disturb you."

"Not at all," said Ivor. "I have my eyes shut and soon I'll be asleep."

Vivienne looked at the big man lying under the duvet on her couch now sound asleep. She shook her head. If only she could fall asleep so easily.

To start with, she did several large circles and saw imaginary blue neon light travelling around both circles. Surely, by tomorrow, she would be able to cut the chords. But walking and imagining the blue light just woke her up even more. There was no point in staying in the lounge, so she decided to walk around the house, being aware, as she walked, of exactly where she was and what she was doing, so that no worrisome thoughts came into her head. She walked around the dining room, then past the kitchen and into her large sleeping area. She looked at her bed, so inviting, with the rose-patterned duvet on it. And the puffy pillows. Feeling a bit like Goldilocks, who tested out the beds, she thought a little rest on the bed was in order.

She lay on the bouncy thick duvet with her head on the soft pillow and without meaning to, fell sound asleep. She half-pulled a bit of the duvet over her body, so she was partly covered and slept for a good long time before the images started. Horrid red and green arms and long-fingered skinny hands with long claws on them, waved towards her throat with screeching voices. She jumped up in fright, calling out as she did … "No you don't!" and jumping onto the floor at the same time.

She stood, shaking her head, bewildered. Also bewildered was the large white snowman, who tumbled into her bedroom. "Vivienne, you called… shouted," he said. "Are you okay?"

Vivienne went over to Ivor and put her head on his shoulder. "I'm both okay and not okay. I can't stand it, Ivor. The visions are so real. So threatening."

Ivor put his arms around her. "It's okay, Vivienne. I'm here and just let me hold you till you feel calm."

"That could be for quite a long time," Vivienne snivelled. "I feel unnerved. Dreadful. I can't go back to sleep, Ivor." She stood with Ivor holding her for a while, then moving out of his arms she said in a wobbly voice, "I'm calm now, or calmer, thanks, Ivor. Let's both sit down on the couch. I'm sorry your sleep got interrupted..."

Together, they went through to the lounge. Ivor pulled his duvet to one side so Vivienne had room to sit next to him. He put his arm tentatively around her and she gratefully relaxed. Neither spoke. For Vivienne, it was comforting to sit with Ivor's protective arm around her. Ivor was looking at her.

Her usually neat hair was tousled. Distress was written all over her face. "Just stay close to me, Vivienne. Remember I'm a big white snowman ready to protect you from evil spirits." And he smiled gently at her. Vivienne sighed and gave a tentative smile back. "If we both fall asleep sitting here," said Ivor, "and those boogie men come and taunt you, I'm right here."

Vivienne nodded and so they both sat, with the duvet tucked around their legs and fell asleep like that. It was an uncomfortable way to sleep, but both were so tired that sleep could not be dismissed.

And, strangely, having a big white snowman with his arm protectively around her did help. Vivienne's fitful sleep was not disturbed by any more malicious entities out to threaten her life. She awoke with a shock, to find Ivor asleep with his head almost on her shoulder, and she smiled to herself. It was almost dawn, and she gently untangled herself from him. She saw him slump across the sofa and continue with his sleep, while she went through to watch the dawn break. She sat, breathing deeply. Just watching the light of day break through the darkness of night. She sat for quite a long time after light had showered the outside scene. And very much later, breathing heavily, she went to the kitchen. That coffee would be good for both of them after a very disturbed night.

The smell of the coffee woke Ivor and she heard his heavy footsteps making for the kitchen. His hair was tousled and he was rubbing his eyes sleepily. He hesitated at the kitchen door. Vivienne felt her spirits lift. There was this big white snowman at the kitchen door with his shaggy beard, which she irreverently thought should also be white, straightening his tousled hair and rubbing his beard.

"Coffee wakes me," he said, the sparkle back in his eyes.

"I thought it might," said Vivienne.

"You been up a long time?" Ivor asked.

150

"Oh yes," said Vivienne. "I watched dawn break, which took quite a while as I wasn't in a hurry. And I hope you got some sleep, anyway."

"Oh yes, I found myself lying across the whole of the sofa. Did I turn you out?"

"No," said Vivienne. "I had a short lovely sleep protected by a white angel." And she smiled at him. "You know, Ivor, that white outfit of yours does have magical or spiritual powers, because I had no more bad dreams when I fell asleep next to you."

"There what did I tell you?" Ivor asked with satisfaction, sitting down to a large cup of coffee. "I know that snow-white track suit was meant for a purpose, but what purpose I didn't know when I bought it."

They both sat, content that the day had started and the dreaded night was over.

"Today," said Vivienne, "I am going to sever the two circles. It is six days now since I've been energizing that blue light around the two circles. And it's time that Maureen looks after her own rubbish and leaves me in peace."

"Agreed," said Ivor, "but I still think I should come here again tonight, just to see that you are okay. It did help, didn't it?"

"Most certainly it did, Ivor and thank you so much. Last night was almost perfect."

"Just one bit of drama," Ivor reminded her with a smile.

"Oh yes, I do remember," said Vivienne, "and this has been a most unpleasant week."

"Then, after this coffee, I'll be off, Vivienne, but will be back again tonight."

"The snowman again," quipped Vivienne.

"I think so," said Ivor. "I'm not superstitious but white is for purity."

Vivienne, serious now, nodded her head.

"I am hugely grateful, Ivor," she said. "Thank you."

"I'll be off then," he said, getting up.

Vivienne stood up as well to unlock the back door for him. As he left, he gave her an affectionate hug.

"This will soon be forgotten, something of the past," he said as he left.

Vivienne heard his car start and drive off. She wasn't so sure that everything would be alright and she had the strangest feeling that a visit to Lady Lavender was what they both needed. Ivor had opened up so much in these nights he'd spent with her, but there was more, she was sure. And she wanted Lady Lavender to help her clear the last of Maureen out of her aura, or whatever she had psychically attached herself to.

Which reminds me, thought Vivienne, I have that cutting ceremony to deal with.

She felt it was a ceremony. One in which she would take the sharpest knife that she had and make a clean cut at the point where the two circles just touched each other. She felt shivers go up her spine.

Would bad entities attack her? She pushed the thought away. Stay in the moment, Vivienne she said to herself. You are in the kitchen just planning. No need to jump ahead. Perhaps calm down and wash the coffee cups, she told herself. So, she did, drying them and being aware of what she was doing.

Perhaps she told herself, I had better shower and put on clean clothes, so that I am the least contaminated with stray entities. Twenty minutes later, she was also in a pure white outfit, a pair of white trousers and a white t-shirt. She even put on white socks and white takkies. Silly, she thought and then another thought, no not silly at all, just taking precautions.

In the kitchen she found the sharpest knife she had. Taking a deep breath, she went from the kitchen into the lounge, and stood close to where the two circles touched. This had to be done correctly. She concentrated hard on what she was about to do, then with the knife she made one swift sure cut at the point where the two circles touched. It was actually so deep that it cut her carpet but this she didn't mind. Her breath flew out of her with a great lift of her spirits.

She smiled as she felt a burden lift and a whooshing sound as the other circle turned in on itself. Her circle remained strong and stable and pure with her own thoughts and high standards. Was it imagination or did she hear a kind of a despairing groan ... the groan of someone who knows at last she had lost the dirty game she was playing?

Vivienne didn't know, but she went to the kitchen to wash her knife and to the bathroom to wash her hands with soap and disinfectant, until she felt there was no vestige of bad vibes on them.

At the same time, she felt that she needed to get out into the sunshine as fast as possible. ... also, to where there was some wind and water... right at the edge of the bay, under the umbrellas where on that first day that little thief had attacked her. But that was soon forgotten. That was the ideal place so she locked the back door and very soon she was across the road and had almost run down the causeway beneath the railway line to reach the outdoor seating area of The Brass Bell...

Chapter 9

Vivienne took in huge breaths of salty air, and listened to the waves as they relentlessly broke against the walls of the restaurant. It was mesmerising, and what with she waves and the wind, and a healthy sun beating down on her, she was soon very much in a new moment, a moment of happiness.

Whilst she was enjoying her happiness and the feeling of freedom, her cell phone rang. It was Steven. Her mind hopped back to her son in Paris. She had not given him that much thought the last couple of days and now felt rather ashamed of herself. She was a mother and her son was in trouble. As she answered the phone, she wondered what his state of mind would be like.

"Hello, Steven," she said cautiously.

"Hello, Mom," said Steven. Vivienne monitored his tone of voice. It was steady. Maybe all was okay.

"How are you, Steven?" she asked.

Steven sighed. "I'm okay, Mom, and how are you?"

Three hours earlier, she would have had a very different reply for him.

"I'm good, thanks, Steven. I'm sitting beside the water at The Brass Bell, enjoying the sound of the sea and the feel of the sun and the wind blowing away all my troubles."

She didn't mean to say this, but Steven reacted. "I wish it was here blowing my troubles away," he said, with fervour.

Vivienne didn't pursue this line of questioning, but waited for Steven to speak. "Mom, about Mariette and the baby, it's got worse as she told her mother and her mother reacted. Not the way, Mariette had hoped, as she is totally against abortion. She hasn't told her father yet. She is dealing with her mother's bad reaction."

Steven paused then said in a rush, "I'm afraid her mother is not pleased with me. Though that's not entirely fair as we both made this baby happen and I'm against it being aborted, too."

Vivienne wasn't going to be drawn into any pros or cons … she still remembered Lady Lavender's stern warning to stay out of her son's business and let him deal with it.

"Well," she said cautiously. "You sound a bit better than last time I spoke to you."

"Well, I'm not," said Steven irritably. "I'm not better at all as Mariette is in a worse state. And she still has to tell her father and goodness knows how he's going to react."

"You might have to come back here," said Vivienne hopefully.

"No chance of that, Mom," said Steven. "I have to face the music here and on top of that I am working well with the firm on this side of the ocean."

Vivienne was quiet. She wasn't going to share any of her recent problems with Steven as they were too many and too complex and too much as if they were from some science fiction movie. Steven was quiet as well, and after a minute or two of saying nothing, he said, "Then Mom, I'll ring off and catch you tomorrow, perhaps."

"Yes, Steven, that is a good idea," she said steadily. "And I do wish you the best of everything in dealing with all of this."

Vivienne heard Steven ring off and gave a great sigh of relief. It wasn't any easier for him, but Vivienne knew she had Mariette's mother on her side. What would her father do? She shuddered slightly. Like Steven said, he had to stay there to face the music.

Vivienne felt her spirits drop as she, in some way, identified herself with Steven and his troubles. Then she remembered Lady Lavender, likening straying thoughts to wild horses. 'Bring them back gently,' she had said, so Vivienne took a deep breath and looked around her. A seagull was busy bobbing in the water, another was swooping over its head, and the drama of their lives took her immediate attention. The gull with the morsel in his or her beak was trying to eat it before the other gull got hold of it. And Vivienne watched this little drama play out.

A child playing near to her accidentally sent a spray of water from his bucket her way and wet her. She jumped, the water was cold and the attack sudden. The child looked unaware and Vivienne shook her head and smiled. Yes, she was back in Kalk Bay sitting on a hard wooden bench under an umbrella next to a family with small children. Her attention went back to the wide expanse of ocean at False Bay with the faint misty hills, or were they mountains on the far distant shore. Such a lovely place to be, she thought, and gave a sigh. Yes, I've spent enough time here, time to get back and clear up the house ... and prepare for tonight. Yes, momentarily, she thought of Ivor in his white track suit and smiled. He did lift her spirits.

Soon she was walking back beneath the railway line and listening to the rumble of wheels as a train passed overhead. Then she was across the street, up her cobbled lane, and climbing the steps to her back door. To her home. Yes, it was home and she was getting to appreciate it more every day.

She spent an hour or more sweeping and tidying and then she went into the lounge. She hesitated as she entered, remembering the two circles she had drawn. But she reminded herself she had severed them and they were not there anymore. Well, she hoped they were not. She didn't mind her circle with herself firmly in the centre. She wondered if she would ever get over the thought of Maureen in her lounge, but knew she needed to clear every bit of Maureen out of her mind and certainly out of her home. Yes, tomorrow, she and Ivor would visit Lady Lavender, who always seemed to have the right things to say to put her feet on firm ground.

Time these days was going faster and soon it was evening and Ivor had arrived.

Again, she had put an array of tasty goodies to nibble on whilst they sat in the lounge. Ivor arrived taking off this overcoat to reveal the white tracksuit, which put a smile on Vivienne's face.

"Hello, Ivor," she said, hugging him. "It's so kind of you to spare time to be with me." She was sincere in what she said.

"I'm enjoying it, Vivienne," said Ivor. "Let's say I was in a rut." And he looked at her and smiled gently. "But you have taken me out of it... the things you get up to Vivienne!" This he said light-heartedly and then immediately amended it. "Of course, I did have some part in it," he admitted, "so I do accept responsibility. But together we will weather this."

Ivor followed her through to the lounge.

"I've swept today," she said, "and vacuumed ... wanted to get as much of the bad stuff out of my house. Do you think the atmosphere is any better?"

"I didn't notice the atmosphere before, but I guess there is a new light feeling in this lounge," he said, looking around him. "Maybe the evil energies have all gone."

"I'm praying they have," said Vivienne fervently. "And I'm longing for a good night in my own bed again,"

159

"Oh, Vivienne, how could you say that?" Ivor teased. "When here I am, this big snowman, ready to protect you."

"It's not the protection, which I appreciate, it's the comfort of stretching out under a feather duvet," Vivienne admitted. "But we are going to see Lady Lavender tomorrow and I'm sure my house and mind will be back on track."

"So that is what we are doing tomorrow?" asked Ivor.

"Yes," said Vivienne. "We both need to see her."

"Then it's just this last night," said Ivor, "then I'm sure we will both go back to normal living. Then he smiled at Vivienne. "But I rather like this," he said, "and do you mind if I eat the crystallised fruit again?"

Vivienne didn't mind, and soon they were chatting comfortably.

Vivienne had again put out small glasses of sherry, to warm them up and relax them. Ivor learnt more about the time Vivienne was a teacher's wife in a house in the country.

"That's where the art teacher gave me a few lessons on how to draw being aware that the blank spaces are also part of a drawing and to leave out what didn't interest me. I just had a few lessons then had fun sketching horses and the river and plants." Ivor had got more insights into Vivienne when he suddenly said, "I'm ready to fall asleep Vivienne, and I wonder if you would like to sit next to me, so I could protect you as I did last night with my arm around you? I liked it and it did help you, didn't it?"

She could see he was hoping for an affirmative.

"It actually did help a lot, Ivor. I slept beautifully. It's not any different to sleeping in a bus, or an aeroplane. You sleep sitting up, so yes, I'm all for it," she said with a warm feeling of happiness.

Imagine being happy in this very room that had troubled her only this morning. But that is what happened. Vivienne dimmed the light and sat close to Ivor on the sofa, while he wrapped his big arm around her shoulders. And like the babes in the wood, they both fell asleep, content that this was the right thing for them both.

Vivienne woke with a start. Ivor had fallen against her and he was heavy. She moved carefully away and smiled as he dropped across the entire sofa. It was already past sunrise and no bad entities had attacked her last night. She felt a sense of relief, but hastened to her bedroom to shower and change then made for the kitchen and put on the coffee. She also got out the toaster and the marmalade and some chicken spread. The coffee smell awoke Ivor and he came, yawning, into the kitchen. He stopped, eyeing the coffee.

"Please sit down," said Vivienne. "There is toast and marmalade, or some chicken spread to take away any hunger pains."

161

Ivor sat, smiling at Vivienne as he buttered some toast and added sugar to his coffee. "Thanks, Vivienne," he said, "then I'll be off immediately."

"You will come back quite soon?" she asked in a worried tone.

"Oh yes. I know it's important for you to see Lady Lavender. I'll be back."

Vivienne didn't add that it was also important for him. She was sure Lady Lavender would help him unearth more of what was currently blocked ...

An hour later, Ivor was walking with Vivienne down the cobbled lane outside her back door. He had taken her arm to make sure she didn't trip over the slightly uneven cobbles. Then they had crossed the street and were walking towards the narrow lane that led across the railway lines and down towards the sea and Lady Lavender's fisherman's cottage. The path was narrow and they walked in single file, with Vivienne reminding herself to not think about the future, but to think only of the moment.

It was difficult, but she managed and was in a fairly cheerful mood as they arrived at the cottage. The roses were still in bloom and Ivor stood next to her as she knocked on the door. There was that eye looking at her through the spy glass, then the door opened and Lady Lavender stood there in her usual long dress, this time patterned in a deep rose pink. The mysterious women had a twinkle in her gimlet eyes and a smile as she let them in.

"I knew you would come," she said. "Hello, Ivor and hello, Vivienne."

"Hello, Lady Lavender," they chorused.

"Then it's to the kitchen first, for that ginger tea, if you wish."

"Yes," said Ivor, "definitely and thank you."

"This time, it's lemon cookies," said Lady Lavender, "made with real lemon. Very refreshing. Please take some," She indicated a large tin of lemon cookies.

Seated in the lounge, with the big black cat policing the scene, Lady Lavender said, "We have a week of your escapades for me to catch up with." She said this with a faint twinkle in her eye.

Both Ivor and Vivienne looked shocked. This had been a dreadful week. Was Lady Lavender making light of it?

"Do sit and taste the cookies," she persuaded. Vivienne and Ivor sat down. Each took a bite of a delicious lemon cookie.

"That's better," said Lady Lavender. "You will see that it's not all that bad. I know you've had a trying week. I've been watching it all happen. But I am not allowed to interfere and, Vivienne, you did magnificently with those two circles."

Vivienne, just finishing a mouthful of lemon cookie, was taken by surprise.

"You know about the circles?" she said.

"Well, I told you to draw them," said Lady Lavender. "And I watched you. You did it perfectly. And it was *perfectly all right to cut them on day six*. You had made them strong enough to stand on their own and yes, you are free now of Maureen ... that is her name, isn't it?"

"Yes," said Vivienne, in awe of what Lady Lavender knew.

"And yes, Vivienne, all of that lady's evil antics have rebounded on her. She is in the nastiest mess anyone could ever wish for. You would do well to keep far away from her."

"I don't need to see her again, do I?" asked Vivienne.

"No, and I know she turned up at Ivor's house," said Lady Lavender with a trace of amusement. "But now Ivor we need to look at you. We know Vivienne is in the clear. You needn't worry, Vivienne, she cannot trouble you psychically again. But there is still stuff Ivor needs to deal with."

"I do," said Ivor in mild shock.

"Yes, Ivor, you do," said Lady Lavender firmly. "Just drink some more of that ginger tea and we will do a small bit of hypnosis and see what the block is because there is a block and I'm sure you are aware of it."

Ivor nodded his head slowly.

"I do agree that I feel there is a gap in my life. Something is missing. Nothing I can be aware of though," he said.

"Well, just relax and enjoy the tea and cookie. You had a good week, I take it?"

"Interesting," said Vivienne, "and very challenging."

"But you stood up to it very well," approved Lady Lavender. She was watching them, Vivienne knew. And though Vivienne felt relieved that she was fee of Maureen she did wonder what Ivor was to reveal.

The sun was shafting though the small windows and Vivienne felt a lift of the spirits. Lady Lavender did this no matter how bad the problem was. Ivor put down his cup and looked at Lady Lavender.

She looked back at him with her gimlet eyes. "Now Ivor, please just relax. Sit as comfortably as you can in that chair and close your eyes. Pretend you are going to sleep. Just breathe deeply and watch your thoughts ... a strange thing will happen. You will find silence in your head and when this happens, keep your eyes shut and concentrate on that silence. Soon, a scene will occur ... just watch the scene. Watch it and be quiet."

Both Ivor and Vivienne sat silently. Vivienne was anxious until Lady Lavender wagged an admonishing finger at her. ... *oh yes, stay in the moment and don't interfere*, thought Vivienne.

Ivor had his eyes shut. "There is a black kind of stage coach," he said. "With horses. And a woman. A woman leaving with bags. Sad to be leaving."

"Just watch her, Ivor," said Lady Lavender.

Ivor watched her. "She had a tearful face as she threw a last glance back and the horse-drawn carriage drew off."

"From an earlier era," said Lady Lavender. "But continue looking, Ivor."

Next, he said he saw a man, dishevelled, angrily turning the furniture over and shouting. His father, perhaps? And a woman, another woman. His mother, perhaps, leaving his father? He wasn't sure. Ivor opened his eyes and related all this to Vivienne and Lady Lavender.

"Keep watching the shifting scenes, Ivor," said Lady Lavender quietly.

Ivor closed his eyes again.

Then Ivor said, "I see myself, blond-haired and young … a teenager. And Maureen. Maureen's green arms are curling around me. I'm in a kind of a witches' coven with drink and drugs." He shuddered.

"What is it," asked Lady Lavender.

"It's terrifying."

"Yes, she had her evil witchcraft working for her even then," said Lady Lavender.

"She is saying, 'You will be my husband. I will make sure of that. You are under my control now and forever.'"

Vivienne saw Ivor shudder.

"Never," he said. "I will never marry."

"There," said Lady Lavender, "now you know the reason you have remained single. Maureen had her evil coils into you from that young age and she has been in your aura ever since."

"Surely not," said Ivor.

"I'm afraid she has," said Lady Lavender.

"And is she still there?"

"To a degree she is," said Lady Lavender.

"Then what am I to do?" said Ivor in horror.

"Not the same as Vivienne, but there is something you can do, which can break these tendrils that are still twirling around you, more so, because she has been thrown back on her own devices and has not got Vivienne to harass ... you are likely to feel very uncomfortable, but not for long, Ivor," said Lady Lavender as Ivor shuddered and opened his eyes,

"We mystics have our own ways of dealing with evil. As she undoubtedly will be sending bad vibes to your house, you need to put salt in each corner of every room and you are to make a hot mixture of these two different lots of herbs I am giving you." And she put on the small table in front of Ivor, two brown paper bags, each marked with a name. "One, you are to drink and the other, you are to inhale, make steam and put your head over and breathe deeply.

"These three actions will clear away any evil she has sent your way, but please be consistent. Start with the herbal drink immediately you get home, and put the salt in each corner of every room immediately. The imbibing of the steam you can do at the start of a new day. as the sun rises. You will chase off any bad spirits with these three magical mixtures."

The sun was lightly shining through the window onto the trio in the lounge. Lady Lavender noticed and said, "Good news! The sun is on your side, Ivor. It has just been blessing all of us."

Ivor, who had been looking very troubled, relaxed a little. He wasn't actually smiling, but Vivienne saw him looking at Lady Lavender and she knew, in his way, he was thanking her.

Lady Lavender noticed, too, and said gently, "Ivor, take heart. You are on your way to a new path in your life." She nodded her head in a kind of dismissal.

Vivienne stood up and thanked her. Ivor followed, and with a small bow to Lady Lavender, he turned and followed Vivienne to the front door.

Soon, they were out in the sunshine and on their way home.

Vivienne held Ivor's arm until the lane got too marrow. She felt he needed reassurance. This wasn't usual for Ivor, a calm stoical kind of man.

Ivor glanced at Vivienne and she caught his eye and smiled, squeezing his hand at the same time. She said nothing. She knew it would show her sense of concern for him, even though she said nothing.

Soon the lane was too narrow and again they went in single file. Then they were in the lane passing Vivienne's back door. Ivor said, "I won't come in, Vivienne. I am anxious to get home and start putting salt in the corners of all my rooms."

Vivienne knew he also meant he needed to drink that herbal concoction, so she nodded her head.

"Lady Lavender knows things we don't know."

"I'll call you tomorrow," said Ivor, "and let you know how things are for me."

"Please," said Vivienne. She didn't add that she was shocked at what Lady Lavender had revealed and heartily hoped he would get those nasty tendrils of Maureen away from his being.

They parted ways and Vivienne watched him go off. Part of her was joyous as she was clear of Maureen, but part of her was concerned for Ivor.

Back inside her house, she made herself a cup of coffee and just sat, doing nothing. Whilst she was sitting the cell phone rang. It was Steven.

He sounded distraught. Oh no, thought Vivienne, no more drama. But Steven started before Vivienne could say anything.

"Mom, Mariette's father threw a fit. He is a very fair man, but with a short temper and often doesn't think before he talks. And this idea of Mariette with a baby knocked him for a six."

"So did he hit you?"

"No, Mom, he's not that kind of violent man," said Steven with dignity. "But he had plenty to say in a very angry voice. Both Mariette and I are in the dog box. And he was even more horrified when he heard she wanted an abortion. He is a moral man and taking a life is not to his way of thinking."

"So Mariette has two parents against her and you as well?"

"You could put it like that only she doesn't see it like that. She is still very emotional and can't talk about it at all."

"So you are in the hot seat," said Vivienne. She felt cheered that both parents were against the abortion. *Who knew what would happen?*

"Steven, you are doing the right thing by staying there and holding fast. Don't annoy her parents. Steven."

"I have annoyed them already," said Steven. "Mariette with a baby is not what they wanted either."

Vivienne didn't want to get further involved so she kept quiet. Steven did as well, so after a period when neither spoke, Vivienne said, "Then let's ring off, Steven, and hold tight. I'll look forward to a call from you, perhaps tomorrow?"

"Sure, Mom," said Steven, "and thanks for your support." He rang off.

Vivienne noticed her coffee was cold. And more than anything, she needed a hot cup of coffee, so she went to the kitchen to heat it up in the microwave. As she did so, she looked around her. Stay in the moment, Vivienne, she said to herself. Never mind Ivor or Steven, you are in this cheerful yellow kitchen with everything you need, she thought. Yes, of course. Best thing to do for her peace of mind was to get out her art materials and to paint or draw something... just to keep her mind quiet and occupied so it didn't start over-thinking. She could so easily do that with all she had been through.

It didn't take long for Vivienne to put out her art materials and once she had paint on her palette and her brush ready, she filled her mind with paint and paper.... She would catch up with Ivor and Steven later.

Chapter 10

Vivienne thought it was wonderful to have a peaceful home and a peaceful night's sleep. She still awoke before dawn and went through to watch the sunrise … then came the routine, shower, and dress, make coffee and have breakfast. She knew Ivor well by now, but still did not want to intrude on his privacy. He would ring her when he was ready.

What to do on this new day? Not paint. She had done that yesterday. Walk, perhaps? She found she had a slight agitation, not surprising with both Steven and Ivor with problems.

Something made her pick up her phone and ring Steven. Time to tell him about Ivor, but not all the drama surrounding Maureen.

Steven answered the phone, sounding weary. "Hi, Mom, what is it?" he asked.

"Steven, I need to tell you. I have made good progress in art."

"I'm pleased, Mom," said Steven.

"But that's not all, Steven. The art teacher and I have a bond now."

"*Bond* - what do you mean, Mom?"

"Just that. Steven. He has become more than a friend." She gave a small embarrassed laugh. "I think I might even be in love, Steven."

172

"Good heavens, you mean I may be getting a stepfather?" Steven laughed.

"You are traversing a new path, Steven and I may be as well. Nothing definite. I'm just telling you how I feel."

"Well, I'm glad for you, Mom," said Steven. "I'm happy you've found someone who makes you happy. I have... or had ..." He hesitated. "Not sure now, Mom, what's happening with Mariette and the baby."

"Her father, Steven?"

"Oh, he's calmed down, Mom. His outbursts don't mean a lot and he's okay now."

"And Mariette's mother?"

"Reasonable, too. She likes me."

Vivienne held her breath.

"And Mariette?"

"That's the problem, Mom, I'm not sure how she feels about me now."

Vivienne opened her mouth to say more, but remembered the MYOB advice and said nothing.

But Steven was in a more cheerful mood as he said, "Your news gives me something to think about ... it's nice Mom, it really is. Tell, me about him."

"Well, he an established artist, who's been tutoring me. We get along really well and he's very supportive of me and my art. So we have that in common."

"He sounds perfect for you, Mom."

Vivienne let out a big breath as he rang off. Whatever had made her phone him and tell him that? It was just a feeling and she was glad she had. Any new developments with Ivor would be easier for him to handle. And she felt sure there would be many.

Best to get on with the day and never mind what was happening to other people. She decided to cook an apple tart, either for dessert or for afternoon tea. So she stayed in the kitchen which was a good place ... she quickly became involved in what she was doing, peeling apples, making pastry, rolling it out, finding cloves to spice up the apples, putting it in a pie case and covering the top with a layer of pasty that she brushed with egg to make it brown in the baking.

It was soon in the oven and delicious smells of baking and apples were in the kitchen. Vivienne smiled. So nice to have a peaceful home and mind again.

She had just washed her hands when she heard the sound of footsteps coming up her back steps. She was pretty sure she knew whose footsteps they were. She had dried her hands and was walking towards the back door when she heard a knock, quite a quick knock, as if someone had something important to say.

She opened the door to see the slightly tense face of Ivor, who immediately smiled when he saw Vivienne.

"Do come in," said Vivienne.

And without much ceremony, Ivor did just that. Came indoors. As soon as he was indoors and Vivienne had shut and locked the door, he startled Vivienne by grabbing her shoulders ... not roughly but with a kind of pent-up excitement.

"What is it, Ivor?" asked Vivienne, leading him towards the lounge.

"Incredible," he said. "You won't believe the difference in the atmosphere in my house. I had noticed a kind of gloomy heaviness, but it's gone. Totally gone. All those saucers of salt I put in all the corners of each room did the trick ... absorbed the bad vibes. The atmosphere in my house is light and airy, Vivienne."

Vivienne had never seen Ivor in this slightly exuberant mood. And excited too. She sat down in a big chair and Ivor claimed the sofa.

"And that's not all, Vivienne," he continued. "I have been drinking that concoction. It's vile, I might tell you, with little leaves and twigs floating about. The point of it was that I needed to vomit and vomit I did ... heartily... horribly ... but that was to take away the evil tendrils Maureen had implanted in me ... I am sure that also has cleared away the fogginess in my mind. That I did last night and, finally, I just did that steaming with the third lot of leaves and my mind is clear now. Clear as day."

He was now sounding joyous and Vivienne had to smile. To have Ivor out of control was a rarity.

"I feel like a free man, a man on a new course, ready to be vulnerable to life's ups and downs. Not to always go in a straight unbending line.

"And Vivienne, this may sound crazy, but..." He stood up and pulled Vivienne to her feet. "I know I have been missing out on the fullness of life ... now I'm talking about you, Vivienne... you have no idea what joy and richness, you have put into my life. I'm not sure how you feel, but I know for me, my life is richer with you in it ... that partner we talked about but maybe more..." He hesitated, and moved slightly back from Vivienne, so he could see her better ... "every day. It might sound crazy from someone my age, but I love you, Vivienne. I really do. I only realised that when I finished steaming myself and my mind went clear. How do you feel about me, Vivienne?"

Vivienne was close to tears. She moved closer to Ivor and put her head on his shoulder. "Oh, Ivor, you cannot know what joy you bring to me. More than anything, I'd love to have you in my life."

"Yes, I am saying that I want you in my life, I do want a wife and I do want to marry you." He drew Vivienne close to him and put his arms around her. Vivienne's heart raced. The feeling of security and happiness she got from this simple action filled her being. They stood together in the lounge, embracing one another. It felt so good, Vivienne's joy knew no bounds. Stay in the moment, she told herself, and this moment is one I would want to last forever...another thought flashed into her head … Lady Lavender had told Ivor he had a new road ahead. For both of them, it would be the perfect thing.

Holding her hand, he guided her to the sofa where they both sat, just looking at one another. Ivor's eyes had that special twinkle back in them. That was when he teased her and she did enjoy it. It kept her from being too serious.

Sit lightly to life, she had once heard.

"We have much to talk about," said Ivor, "but is that apple pie I smell cooking? Is it for any special reason?"

"Of course, I knew you were coming," she said, with a warm smile. "It will be a bit hot as it's just out of the oven, but let's share it."

"And coffee," said Ivor. "I haven't had breakfast today. I was just so overwhelmed with all I was discovering and feeling."

"I'm not cooking breakfast now," said Vivienne, "but apple tart and coffee will fill any hollow. But it's still too hot to eat."

Ivor said, "While we wait for it to cool down, remember, I was to take you painting the old mill at Mowbray… how do you feel about that … say this afternoon… just to steady both of us… to get our feet onto the ground as it were? Right now, I feel I could burst into song, which I never do… but, suddenly, life has opened great vistas for me."

Vivienne was smiling at this suddenly ecstatic man. She put her arms around him and hugged him.

"Is this part of life now?" Ivor asked.

"Yes," said Vivienne, "and when I feel like tousling your hair, which I often do, I shall tousle it," She smiled as she gently ruffled his hair. "You are so special," she said. "You really are." She dropped a kiss on his forehead. He put his hand up to his forehead with a bemused look on his face. Then he very gently kissed her. A soft kiss with so much meaning in it.

They sat there, holding one another, Vivienne feeling great waves of love for this man. She didn't know she could ever feel this happy. Then Ivor, still with his arm around her, gently kissed her again and then whispered, "And how about that apple tart and coffee, Vivienne?"

Vivienne laughed and removed herself from Ivor's arms. "Right, you can follow me to the kitchen if you like, and take the apple tart and cream into the lounge whilst I get the coffee sorted."

As they both sat eating apple pie with cream and drinking Vivienne's special brand of coffee, they glanced at one another. A new chapter in life would soon be starting for each of them.

When the apple tart and coffee break was finished, Ivor said, "Let me be off and I'll be back in the car to pick you up in, say, two hours' time, Vivienne... there is still plenty of time to get a painting done."

Vivienne watched the look on his face. It was relaxed and happy and there was that twinkle in his hazel eyes. She shook her head and a warm feeling of love coursed through her as he gave a last wave and went out through the door.

Vivienne spent the next two hours in a dream-like state, getting her art materials ready with a feeling of awe. Was all this really happening to her? She shook her head and concentrated on getting everything into her basket she kept for art materials. Paints, water jar, cloth, palette brushes and paper.

She thought briefly of the Mowbray windmill. She had seen pictures of it and it had intrigued her. Now to visit it in person and to paint it, creatively ... it may not look much like the windmill when she had finished. This practical application of getting things ready did steady her and, by the time Ivor arrived, she felt in control of herself.

However, when she greeted Ivor today, it was different. She bent forward as she settled herself in the car and indicated that he should kiss her. He bent his head forward. They kissed then smiled at one another, in a kind of self-satisfied way. Ivor held her eyes briefly as he started the car and she saw that mischievous gleam in them. Her good friend would soon be her husband. *How amazing was that!*

Ivor started the car, and Vivienne leaned back. The wind in the open car cooled her cheeks and whipped her hair about and she knew a delicious feeling of happiness. She really loved Ivor and was so glad he returned the feeling. She smiled as they drove along the busy streets to find the old mill at Mowbray.

The grounds were pleasant and open to visitors. Vivienne put down her basket of painting equipment and did a slow tour of the big old building, a chucky white windmill that still operated today. She found an aspect that pleased her, with the arms of the windmill slightly to one side and indicated to Ivor that was where she would work. Ivor had brought two folding chairs and a small folding table which he set up for them. He wasn't going to paint, he said, but would just rest and enjoy being there.

Vivienne nodded. He had been through a lot the past twenty-four hours and rest in a peaceful place was probably what he needed most. Vivienne spent some time just looking at the sky, at the old windmill, at the light and shadows, and the brilliant green grass ... when a slight jerk of her body told her that she was ready to paint.

In a very short time, she had puddles of paint on her palette and had loosely painted the blue sky with clouds, had left a big white space for the old windmill and had loosely painted green grass. To her the most fascinating part of the windmill were the four blades. For these she used the rigger brush with its long slender point. She was very careful in this part of the painting, but after fifteen minutes of intense concentration, she sat back with a satisfied smiled. "It's got character, don't you think, Ivor?" she said to the man dozing next to her.

Ivor sat up with a jerk, blinked, looked at Vivienne's painting and nodded in agreement. "Yes, it's not exactly like the windmill," he said, with that twinkle in his eye, "but one would recognize it as such ... and probably agree it was the old Mowbray windmill."

"Thank you, Ivor. I take that as a compliment," said Vivienne. She felt entirely comfortable sitting next to him and relaxed in her chair. "This is such a special day and this painting just tops it all off ... thank you, Ivor, for bringing me here."

Ivor just nodded, acknowledging her thanks. They were settling their things in the car when her cell phone rang. Vivienne jumped. Not bad news at the end of such a lovely day ... she knew it would be Steven.

In a very cautious voice, she answered the phone. "Hello, Steven," she said, and paused.

"Hello, Mom," said Steven. Vivienne assessed his tone, and breathed a sigh of relief.. it sounded normal.

"Well, Steven, how is it going?" she ventured.

"You'll never guess. Mom, but Mariette heard some horrific things about the effects of abortion on both the unborn foetus, which is cut into pieces, which has a heartbeat, and can feel pain, and the subsequent psychological effect on the mother ... it has quite stunned her." And he had a soft tone to his voice, "Now she isn't so sure about getting an abortion." Then he whispered, "I even saw her looking at pictures on the internet of cots and baby strollers and cribs." Then even more softly … "and I saw her looking at baby clothes, so I am sure she's coming round."

"And that is great news, Steven," said Vivienne, "but what does she feel about *you*… is she still angry?"

"No, Mom, she isn't… Mariette really loves me, and I love her. And Mom, it is all going to be alright." He said this in a joyous tone of voice.

Vivienne, who had been holding her breath, let it out and said warmly, "I'm so glad, Steven. You are so kind and you deserve the best. As does Mariette," she hastened to say. "So I'm happy for both of you."

As Steven was about to ring off, she halted him. One arm was holding onto Ivor for support, as she said, "I have new for you, too, Steven. Ivor has asked me to marry him."

Steven gave a chortle of laughter.

"So I'm to have a stepfather, Mom… is he nice?"

"Oh yes, he is very nice, and he's standing right here. Would you like to say hello to him?"

"Not really, Mom," said Steven, "but all right."

Ivor was listening to all of this, and had his usual twinkle in his eyes as he took the phone from Vivienne, who had put it on loudspeaker.

"Hello, Steven," he said. "I feel I know you as your mother speaks so highly of you. I'm Ivor by the way."

"Her painting tutor, I understand," said Steven.

"Yes, I was that to begin with, but, right now, I guess you could say she is my fiancée."

Steven seemed nonplussed, but, nevertheless, was able to say with real warmth, "I'm so happy for my mom. She's the best and deserves the best."

"I'll do my best to keep her happy," said Ivor.

"Thank you," said Steven and rang off.

Vivienne put her arms around Ivor. "Thank goodness that's over," she said. "I really wasn't looking forward to telling Steven, but he is okay with having a stepfather." She looked at Ivor and smiled...

Printed in the United States
by Baker & Taylor Publisher Services